Lying in Ambush . . .

The mare's slight hesitation of movement and the snort that exploded from her nostrils caused Longarm to glance from side to side just as the man he instantly recognized as Carl Whitfield and another smaller man jumped up with rifles.

"Ya!" Longarm shouted, bending low in the saddle and sending the mare into a hard run in order to escape this death trap. "Ya!"

The mare shot forward like a cannonball, ears flattening against her head, neck stretched out, and legs reaching out to cover ground. The ambushers were caught by surprise, unprepared for the mare's explosive burst of speed. They both fired and missed.

Longarm drew his six-gun and opened fire, emptying his gun at the closer and larger target, Carl Whitfield. The liveryman staggered, dropped his rifle, and collapsed even as his partner fired a shot that struck Longarm high up in the back and nearly knocked him from his saddle.

"Ya!" Longarm shouted, dropping his gun and desperately grabbing for his saddle horn.

The buckskin mare ran like the wind and Longarm heard one last rifle shot, then he was out of range and hanging on for his life.

TABOR EVANS

LONGARM

AND THE GRAND CANYON MURDERS

JOVE BOOKS, NEW YORK

THE BERKLEY PUBLISHING GROUP
Published by the Penguin Group
Penguin Group (USA) Inc.
375 Hudson Street, New York, New York 10014, USA
Penguin Group (Canada), 90 Eglinton Avenue East, Suite 700, Toronto, Ontario M4P 2Y3, Canada
(a division of Pearson Penguin Canada Inc.)
Penguin Books Ltd., 80 Strand, London WC2R 0RL, England
Penguin Group Ireland, 25 St. Stephen's Green, Dublin 2, Ireland (a division of Penguin Books Ltd.)
Penguin Group (Australia), 250 Camberwell Road, Camberwell, Victoria 3124, Australia
(a division of Pearson Australia Group Pty. Ltd.)
Penguin Books India Pvt. Ltd., 11 Community Centre, Panchsheel Park, New Delhi—110 017, India
Penguin Group (NZ), 67 Apollo Drive, Rosedale, Auckland 0632, New Zealand
(a division of Pearson New Zealand Ltd.)
Penguin Books (South Africa) (Pty.) Ltd., 24 Sturdee Avenue, Rosebank, Johannesburg 2196,
South Africa

Penguin Books Ltd., Registered Offices: 80 Strand, London WC2R 0RL, England

This is a work of fiction. Names, characters, places, and incidents either are the product of the author's imagination or are used fictitiously, and any resemblance to actual persons, living or dead, business establishments, events, or locales is entirely coincidental

LONGARM AND THE GRAND CANYON MURDERS

A Jove Book / published by arrangement with the author

PRINTING HISTORY
Jove edition / February 2012

Copyright © 2012 by Penguin Group (USA) Inc.
Cover illustration by Milo Sinovcic.

ISBN: 978-0-515-15037-7

JOVE®
Jove Books are published by The Berkley Publishing Group,
a division of Penguin Group (USA) Inc.,
375 Hudson Street, New York, New York 10014.
JOVE® is a registered trademark of Penguin Group (USA) Inc.
The "J" design is a trademark of Penguin Group (USA) Inc.

PRINTED IN THE UNITED STATES OF AMERICA

10 9 8 7 6 5 4 3 2 1

Chapter 1

Deputy United States Marshal Custis Long stepped into the office of his boss and friend, Chief Marshal Billy Vail, and said, "Whatever it is you want me to do . . . I'm unavailable."

Billy was of medium size and today exhibited an unflappable and sunny disposition, no doubt due to the fact that he was now in charge of their federal office and mostly handled paperwork and personnel assignments. "Have a chair, Custis."

Longarm knew that he was being baited into a trap and shook his head. "Billy, I just returned from a month in the damned desert near Yuma, where I was stuck by cactus, bit by a scorpion . . . twice . . . and damned near died of thirst and heat exhaustion. The killer I was after somehow managed to get a rattlesnake in my boot while I slept; I barely escaped getting bitten before I shot the snake *and* the demented killer who was waiting to see me die of snakebite. I'm telling you that my last assignment was a nightmare, so unless you have something easy for me to do in the cool mountains, I'm unavailable."

"Would you like a really good cigar? I have a few special Cubans."

Longarm groaned. "This is looking worse by the minute. But I won't be bribed so easily, because I just met a really interesting lady that I'm very interested in spending a lot of time with."

"You're *always* meeting an interesting lady, aren't you?" Billy grinned and gave his favorite deputy a manly wink. "A new flame every week or two. Always lovely, always passionate, always a brief love affair. Custis, you need to find a woman that is like my wife. Solid. Dependable. Not flashy or witty, but just salt of the earth and one that will stand by you through thick and thin."

"Given the pittance this office pays me as an excuse for a salary," Longarm muttered grumpily, "for me times are always thin."

"Oh now, it isn't that bad. So cheer up, because I've just heard that we're going to get a federal pay raise this fall."

"I've heard that from you every year I've worked here, and it ain't happened yet."

"Ahh," Billy said, raising a forefinger from behind his massive walnut desk. "But I am considering you for a *field promotion.*"

"And I've heard that before too."

Billy smiled and shook his head as if it were a trial to deal with such a gifted but obstinate deputy marshal. "Sit down, Custis. And do take one of these Cubans and enjoy yourself with me for a little while. We have something very exciting and important on our plate."

Longarm took a seat in front of Billy's desk and snatched a long, black cigar from the humidor. His eyes fell on the cigar and he sniffed it with suspicion, knowing that sometimes Billy claimed he smoked Cubans but they were actually cheap Mexican imitations. "All right," Longarm said, satisfied that the cigar was as claimed, "what is it you're trying to hook me into this time?"

"We have a disappearance," Billy said. "A strange and troubling one . . . actually *two* disappearances."

"People disappear all the time. Sometimes they have very good and rational reasons to disappear. Too much debt. A nagging wife. A lovely mistress or an enemy that is trying to put them in the ground. Why, I once even heard of a man who disappeared because he couldn't stand all of his wife's cats."

"Those are trivial reasons for disappearing. I'm talking about two very important and responsible people," Billy said, striking a match and then lighting both of their cigars. "And their disappearances took place in an extremely unique setting."

"Don't tell me . . . They disappeared in Death Valley."

"No," Billy said with a chuckle. "Some place even more remote and dangerous."

"Alaska Territory?" It would be good to go there now, Longarm thought, before wintertime set in up in that cold, lonesome country.

"Uh-uh. The location I'm talking about is much, much closer to us here in Denver. But it's a place that few have seen. A landscape filled with extreme danger and great mystery."

Longarm realized he was leaning forward in his chair, eager to learn about this mystery. But he wasn't one to be taken in easily, so he leaned back, puffed on his cigar, and said, "The new woman in my life is named Heidi . . . Miss Heidi Zalstra."

"Irish?" Billy asked, trying to be humorous.

"No," Longarm scoffed. "She's a Scandinavian beauty."

"A Swedish girl?"

"Dutch. I believe that is from Holland, where they have those funny windmills everywhere and lots of dikes to hold back water from the sea."

Billy grinned. "Does she wear wooden shoes and say 'Ya' to everything you say?"

Longarm scowled. "Hell, no! She talks like the rest of us and hasn't said 'Ya' to anything I've asked . . . but that is about to change starting *tonight*."

"Tsk, tsk," Billy said, clucking his tongue. "I just can't imagine you and some poor Dutch girl having a lasting relationship. You're not a bit interested in dikes or windmills . . . are you?"

"Of course not, but you can't imagine me having a lasting relationship with *any* woman."

"True." Billy smoked thoughtfully for a moment and then abruptly changed the subject. "How do you feel about water?"

"It can ruin a good glass of whiskey."

Billy didn't smile. "You know that's not what I meant."

"Then speak your mind plainly, Boss."

"Can you swim?"

Longarm gave his boss a queer look. "Why are you askin' me something like *that*?"

"Can you?"

"Yeah. In fact, when I was a country boy in West Virginia, we'd have a Fourth of July parade and then a picnic by the lake. I not only won the footraces, but I was always the fastest kid to swim across the lake and back. I kicked some kid's ass for trying to pin on me the nickname the Flying Duck."

"Yeah, I can see where that would be a bad one. But the fact that you are an excellent swimmer settles it," Billy said with a look of satisfaction.

"Settles what?"

"You're the only one that I'd feel comfortable sending on this extremely important assignment."

Longarm was growing exasperated by Billy's beating-around-the-bush tactics, but he knew better than to press the issue, so he bent his knee over his leg, leaned back in the chair, and smoked the excellent Cuban cigar as if it were the only thought on his mind.

"Well?" Billy asked. "Will you do it?"

"I told you I needed some time to rest up from that desert trip that damn near got my brains fried. Send someone else in the office. Send ole Jasper White."

"Deputy White couldn't even find his way to water, much less swim roaring rapids."

"What about Clyde Hunsitter?"

"He's afraid of water and he recently got his girlfriend pregnant. He's going to marry Betty next week if she doesn't drop it first. I can't send him just now, and even if I did, he'd get himself killed on this assignment."

"That dangerous, huh?"

"Yeah," Billy said. "And you're the only man in this office that has a ghost of a chance of success. Interested?"

"I'm still sitting here, aren't I?"

"Because of that excellent cigar."

"That too," Longarm admitted. "So what is the assignment, or am I supposed to go out and find a swami with a crystal ball to tell me?"

"All right," Billy said, lowering his voice as if someone could actually hear through his closed door. "This one is really, really important and special."

"You always say that."

"I know." Billy held up his hands palms forward, as if making a big confession. "But this time it's the truth."

"Don't matter because I ain't goin', but you can tell me anyway."

"A federal judge and his wife are missing."

Longarm just shrugged his broad shoulders. "Big deal."

"It *is* a big deal! This particular federal judge is related to the President of the United States."

"Then he's probably retarded."

"Dammit, Custis. Be serious!"

"I am."

"Federal Judge Milton Quinn's name is often brought up as a future member of the Supreme Court."

Longarm scowled and blew a smoke ring. "Billy, I don't care if he is the king of Siam. I ain't goin' anyplace for a while."

"And," Billy was saying, "he is rich and generous."

"So now you're trying to say that if I can find and save this Quinn fella and his wife, I will be richly rewarded?"

"I didn't say that."

"I know you didn't actually say that, but that's what you implied. Billy, you know that we can't take money as a reward or bribe."

"There are many ways other than money that a man as important as Judge Quinn can reward those who help him, but I'll not talk about that right now."

"Good," Longarm said, "because you'd be just whistling up a creek with me." Longarm came to his feet. "Mind if I smoke this on my way to the barbershop so I can get a fresh shave for tonight's date with Miss Zalstra?"

"You're not going anywhere just yet," Billy said, the friendliness leaving his voice. "Sit back down while I tell you where you are going as soon as we can make the arrangements."

Longarm sat, but he wasn't happy about it.

"Judge Quinn and his new wife, a much younger woman, have gone to the Arizona Territory . . . more specifically, to the headwaters of the Grand Canyon. To some place called Lees Ferry."

"It's an old Mormon Colorado River crossing. I've been there, and at this time of the year it'll still be hotter than hell."

"The judge and his wife's intentions were to spend their honeymoon on the Colorado River of the Grand Canyon."

Longarm removed the cigar from his lips and studied it a minute. "Are you trying to tell me that the judge and his bride were planning to *boat* through the Grand Canyon like Major John Wesley Powell and some others that came along afterward?"

"That's exactly what I'm trying to tell you," Billy Vail said. "And guess what?"

"They capsized in wild rapids and drowned."

"Partly right."

Longarm sighed. "Why don't you start at the beginning, Billy?"

"Well, there isn't much else that I know. It seems that the bride, one Mavis Henshaw now Mavis Quinn, was the daughter of a Mississippi River steamboat captain. She reportedly met the judge on a trip down the Mississippi to New Orleans, and they fell in love during the Christmas holidays."

"How old is the judge?"

"Fifties, I'd expect, and his new wife is in her twenties and quite stunning. Anyway, Mrs. Quinn had early on developed a love of water and rivers, and she became quite enamored with the idea of running wild rivers. I understand that she had boated down some big rivers, but the great challenge was always the Colorado River through the Grand Canyon."

"So she talked this lovesick fool of a judge twice her age to go with her on this crazy expedition?"

"Yes. I wouldn't doubt that Mavis Quinn can be exceedingly persuasive."

"Yeah, I'll bet. And I'll bet the judge has had such a hard one since he met her that it has caused a lack of blood flow to his brain, so that is why he agreed to this foolish honeymoon trip."

Billy allowed himself a faint smile. "There might be some truth in that. However, it should be said that there are now numbers of boats that regularly take tourists through the Grand Canyon, always wearing floatation devices, and the trips are incredibly expensive and dangerous. Just the sort of combination of dangerous but exciting adventure that would attract young and well-to-do people such as Mrs. Mavis Quinn like moths to a flame."

"Only instead of the moth getting torched, these idiots drown."

"Surprisingly," Billy said, "very few do. I've been told on good authority that the boats that take rich tourists through the Grand Canyon are made for that river and handled by experts; they are far more suited to the rapids than Major Powell's four inadequate wooden boats he used back in 1869."

Longarm had never been down into the Grand Canyon, but he'd seen the Colorado at flood stage when it came out of the canyon, and he'd also seen it disappear into the great chasm up near the border of southwest Colorado. It was, he knew firsthand, a river not to be trifled with or taken lightly. It was a river that demanded great respect.

"Billy, what *exactly* would have me do?"

"I'd like you to go to Lees Ferry and find out if Judge Quinn and his wife actually got on a boat to take them through the Grand Canyon."

"Didn't someone reliable see them depart from Lees Ferry?"

"Apparently not."

"That doesn't make sense."

"Well, what I'm told is that the expedition was making ready for the perilous journey. Two boats, three experienced river navigators, and a half ton of provisions were being readied. But then, one morning, a boat was missing and so were the judge and his wife."

"Just vanished?"

"Just vanished," Billy said with a solemn expression on his round face. "There was no sign of foul play."

"Were provisions missing?"

"Yes."

"Then that crazy bride must have talked the judge into her madness and they went on alone," Longarm reasoned.

"That could be the case. There could also be other reasons to explain the disappearance of such a prominent couple."

"The reasons being?"

"The Quinns were wealthy. They probably had a lot of cash and some expensive gold jewelry. They could have been murdered and dumped into the river then an empty boat set free with a few provisions to make it look as if the couple had foolishly struck out on their own."

"Hmmm," Longarm mused. "That would be a possibility all right. How long have the couple been missing?"

"Approximately one week." Billy leaned forward on

his desk. "Custis, the request to send my best man comes from the very highest sources. Right from the top of the political heap."

"From the President himself?"

Billy nodded.

"Maybe you should go," Longarm said. "It would be a real feather in your hat."

"I can't swim worth a damn," Billy confessed. "And anyway my wife would have none of that. I've got three mouths to feed now."

Longarm sighed. "I know. I know."

"I'm asking you to do this as a personal favor. My career. *Your* career. The reputation of this office hangs in the balance. If you go to Lees Ferry and somehow find the couple still alive, it will be a tremendous boost to all of our careers."

"And if I go and find out that they really were crazy enough to go down that river by themselves without an experienced riverboat guide?"

"Then that is something we have to find out."

Longarm blew a smoke ring up in the air. "Boss, I have to tell you that the most likely outcome is bad. Either the couple was murdered . . . or they went off in a boat and soon drowned. In each of those cases, it's damned unlikely that their bodies will ever be found."

"I'm aware of that but hoping it's not going to be the case. In any event, I've been ordered to launch an investigation from this office and you are the only one of us that can pull it off. Will you do it for me?"

"Billy . . ."

"Will you do it for not only me but yourself and the reputation of this office, and for Judge Quinn and his bride?"

"Ah, Billy, I . . ."

"And for a month's paid vacation and a promise in writing that you'll have both a raise and a promotion?"

"No matter what the outcome?"

"No matter what the outcome," Billy promised.

Longarm came to his feet. He was a tall man and a strong one, but the idea of getting in a boat and going through the Grand Canyon seeking corpses washed up on some sandy shore was very disturbing.

"I'm going to piss off Miss Zalstra."

"I'll invite her to my home for dinner and fill her mind with heroic stories of the deeds you have done as a federal officer of the law."

"You'll tell her about the time I fought three men barehanded in a bear's cave in the Tetons and whipped them all?"

"Oh yeah, and I'll tell them of the time you were in Monument Valley and had to track down six murderers and save that beautiful Mexican girl named . . ."

"Best not tell her about that one," Longarm advised.

"I'll tell her all the good stories," Billy vowed. "By the time my wife and I finish, she'll believe that you are a Nordic god and she'll be panting with anticipation for your return."

"Could work."

"Then you'll do it?"

Longarm jammed the Cuban cigar into his mouth. "A raise in pay. Promotion. You talk me up to Miss Zalstra?"

"All of those things I swear on my mother's grave."

"Last I heard she was still alive, Billy."

"All right, on my father's grave, and that bastard is definitely dead."

"Fair enough!" Longarm extended his massive paw across the desk, and it dwarfed Billy's small, soft hand. "We got a deal. Put it all down in writing and I'll sign it."

Billy's broad smile faded. "In writing?"

"Sure! Any problem with that, Boss?"

"None at all," Billy said weakly. "But I'll want you to leave as soon as possible."

"Tomorrow," Longarm said. "Have my travel funds ready and waiting in the morning. Two hundred ought to do 'er."

"Two hundred? That's a hell of a lot of money, Custis. Lees Ferry can't be that far from Denver."

"Oh, it's far enough," Longarm said. "But if I need to hire a boat and boatman to get me through that monster canyon, I want to hire the best that's available and that won't come cheap."

Billy, who was always tight on the office's budget, sighed and said, "No, I suppose not."

Longarm headed for the door. "Don't forget to have those promises in writing and have the two hundred dollars in cash ready and waiting for me in the morning."

"Have fun with Miss Zalstra tonight."

"Damn right I will!" Longarm called over his broad shoulder as he hurried out the door.

Chapter 2

Longarm got a haircut and went shopping for a few hours. He bought a box of chocolates for Heidi and then hurried to the Broadmore Hotel, where she was staying. It was one of Denver's nicest hotels, in a very good neighborhood, and it reminded Longarm that Miss Heidi Zalstra seemed to have an unlimited source of income. She didn't work and had only been in town a few weeks when he'd met her by chance one Sunday afternoon strolling alongside the banks of Cherry Creek. Although the day had been warm, their paths had fatefully crossed just when the sun was setting over the towering Rockies. The light had been fair, the evening beginning to cool, and folks were out enjoying a little exercise during the most pleasant part of the day.

Heidi had been feeding the ducks that frequented the creek and were so popular to the citizens. Children played, dogs barked and chased balls, and the sunset had begun to christen the highest western peaks. Longarm had been at loose ends, and so when he saw the strikingly beautiful young woman unescorted by any other gentleman, he'd just naturally gone to her and struck up a conversation. And although they had nothing in common, things had gone so well that he'd begun to see her at every opportunity.

Now, as he stood at the door of her hotel room holding the chocolates, he wondered where they would go for dinner and what might transpire afterward. He would, of course, explain everything to her about having to leave on such short notice, and he'd make it clear that he wanted to resume their relationship as soon as he returned from the Grand Canyon.

"Ah, Custis," she said brightly. "Good to see you again!"

"Likewise. I know that you love chocolates, and these are the best to be found in Denver."

"How thoughtful of you," Heidi said, ushering him inside. "Would you like something to drink before we go out to dinner?"

Heidi liked champagne and French Chardonnay wine, but she had started to keep a very good brand of whiskey on hand for his enjoyment. "Sure."

She removed his hat and gave him a kiss on the lips, then hurried into her kitchen to pour them drinks. Longarm took a seat on an expensive but uncomfortable white couch and considered how he would broach the subject of his departure on tomorrow's train. Should he tell Heidi right away, or would he perhaps be better off telling her at the tail end of the evening and hoping that she would be so distraught that she would throw herself into his arms and take him to her bed? Longarm considered this to be a difficult and dicey decision not to be taken lightly.

"Well," Heidi said, bringing Longarm two fingers of Old Kentucky whiskey, "how was your day?"

"Not bad."

"I see you got a fresh haircut and shave."

"Just hours ago, Heidi. And how was your day?" Longarm took a drink, admiring how fine she looked in a pink silk skirt and satin blouse, with a matching ribbon in her beautiful blond hair. She was wearing a stunning gold necklace and a dinner ring of at least a one-carat diamond surrounded by blood-red rubies. The ring alone probably had cost Heidi more than Longarm's annual salary. He took his eyes off of her jewels and asked, "What did you do?"

Heidi sipped her champagne and looked into his gray eyes. "I was offered a very good job at the big jewelry story on Colfax, only a block away from your office."

"Johnson's Jewelry?"

"That's the one."

"It's where anyone with money buys their jewelry," Longarm told her. "I doubt they carry anything in the store that sells for less than a couple hundred dollars."

"I suppose that's true. They want me to be a buyer and appraiser of precious stones."

"Did you accept the job offer?"

Heidi pursed her full lips. "Actually, I was thinking I might take their offer and after a time learn enough about the business to open my own jewelry store next year. I feel that Johnson's is overpriced for what they sell."

"I wouldn't know about that," Longarm admitted. "I've never really been inside the place."

"You don't like jewelry?" Heidi asked with real interest and an amused smile.

"Oh, I like jewelry fine on a woman. But I've seen men that have worn two or three rings and that looks a little . . . ah, fey . . . to me. But I do appreciate a fine pocket watch and chain on a man."

"Your watch and chain are very handsome," Heidi said. "And if you would like to wear a gold or silver ring . . . I could do that."

"Do what?" Longarm asked, not sure if he understood.

"Buy you a ring." Heidi laughed. "It would be fun!"

Longarm laughed too, but it wasn't all that funny. "I'm fine," he said. "I don't need to wear a ring."

"Suit yourself," Heidi told him, looking a little disappointed. "But that was why I went into Johnson's Jewelry."

"To buy *me* something?"

"Why not? You've taken me out to dinner several times, and now you've bought me a lovely box of chocolates. I wanted to repay you, Custis."

"I could probably think of a better way to repay me," he said, looking straight into her wide-set blue eyes. "And it wouldn't cost you a thing."

Heidi was in her early thirties and not a naïve woman. She smiled and sipped her champagne then turned her attention back to him and said, "I know what you want, and it *would* cost me something. Something perhaps more valuable than a man's ring."

"Your virginity?"

She blinked, and he immediately regretted the boldness of his question. But Heidi did not get angry or frustrated. "You know, Custis, I never told you that I was married very briefly to a man in New York City."

"You were?"

"It was a sad and short-lived marriage," she said. "The man I married was handsome and quite wealthy. Arthur came from a prominent family, and I thought we would remain husband and wife for many, many years . . . until one of us passed. Unfortunately, my love was also seeing another woman . . . a married woman . . . and three weeks after we returned from our European honeymoon tour, he was caught in the other woman's bed and shot by her husband, who was even richer than Arthur."

"Arthur was your philandering husband?"

"Yes, the late Mr. Arthur P. Buckingham."

"How come your name isn't Mrs. Heidi Buckingham?"

"The Buckingham family was mortified by the circumstances of Arthur's sudden and unsavory ending. Fearful of a terrible scandal and of their good name being tarnished beyond repair, they offered me a very sizable settlement and a lawyer to effect an immediate annulment of the marriage. In return, I had to sign away any rights to the Buckingham fortune."

"So you did?"

"Not at first. You see, I had an astute lawyer who was paid on a percentage basis, and he squeezed out every dollar that he possibly could from the Buckingham family. I am, Custis, quite a wealthy woman."

She swallowed her glass of champagne and went for a refill.

"I'll also have another," he called, draining his whiskey and trying to rapidly process the ramifications of what he'd just learned. He had, of course, known that Heidi had plenty of money, but he now realized that she was far wealthier than he'd imagined. So why was this rich and beautiful woman even bothering with a poorly paid federal marshal such as himself?

Heidi returned with his glass and sat down next to him. "You know, Custis, I didn't intend to tell you about my past circumstances until we got to know each other much better."

He understood her concern and was not insulted in

the least. "You mean until you could trust me not to be interested in your money instead of yourself."

"That too," Heidi admitted. "Men do go after women for their money."

"True, but when the woman looks as beautiful as yourself, money is pretty much the last thing on their minds. Trust me on that one."

She laughed. "And the foremost thing on your mind is us going to bed?"

"Actually, yes."

"I love your honesty." She placed her glass down on the end table and kissed his mouth, but when he tried to embrace her, Heidi slipped away, saying, "Let's go out to dinner because I'm famished."

Longarm nodded. "All right, but . . ."

"But what?" she asked.

"I have something important that I have to tell you, and since you made your past known to me so honestly, I'm going to tell you that I'm leaving Denver for the Grand Canyon on tomorrow's train."

"Are you serious?" she asked, smile dying.

"I'm afraid that I am. A prominent couple is missing at a place called Lees Ferry, which is on the eastern end of the Grand Canyon. Apparently, the couple planned to hire boatmen to take them through the Grand Canyon and they've completely vanished."

"In the river?"

Longarm shrugged. "No one saw them leave. No one knows exactly where they went or how they disappeared. The couple is related to the President of the United States and they are extremely prominent in Washington, D.C., so my boss is under a lot of pressure."

"And it has to be you who goes to solve this mystery?"

"I'm the best choice," Longarm said. "And I can swim."

Her eyes grew round with amazement. "Are you supposed to *swim* in the Grand Canyon?"

"No," he said, "but I'm sure that there are some wicked rapids, and there is always the danger of being tossed into the water." He took another taste of Old Kentucky and smacked his lips with approval. "Excellent whiskey, Heidi. As good as it comes."

"Yes," she said, "I want you to have the very best. But let's get back to this issue of you leaving tomorrow and going into the Grand Canyon, which I understand is a wondrous and beautiful place but remote and deadly."

"It is that."

"Why don't you refuse to go and stay here with me?" Heidi said, moving closer. "I think we could have something very special together if we had some time."

"Maybe you're right," he told her, "but I have a job."

"Quit the job! I'll take care of you until you find something that you like better."

"There probably isn't anything I'd like better than what I'm doing right now."

Heidi got up suddenly. "Do you really mean that?"

"I'm afraid that I do, Heidi."

She shook her head, suddenly looking troubled. "Custis, I can help you become something much more than a federal marshal."

This time he was insulted. "I'm proud of what I do, and if you—"

Heidi sat right down in his lap. She kissed his mouth and whispered, "Why don't we talk about this some other time?"

"And go to dinner."

She kissed his cheek, then nibbled at his earlobe. "I

just thought of something a little more . . . *physical* . . . than dinner."

"Your bed?" he asked, hardly daring to believe how fast this conversation was turning first one way and then the next.

"Uh-huh."

Longarm placed his whiskey down with a thump and scooped Heidi up in his strong arms. "I know where the bedroom is," he said with a broad grin. "And as for the not being a virgin, I'm happy about that."

"You are?"

"Yes."

"But I thought . . ."

"Never mind what you thought," he said, brushing through the bedroom door and placing her on the bedspread. "Show me how the very rich make love."

"I'm sure we do it just like the poor," she told him as she began to undress. "But perhaps a little slower."

"I'm not going to be slow this time," he confessed. "But I'll be as slow as you want the next."

"The next?"

"Yep."

"And how soon do you suppose that will be?"

"It'll be within the hour," he vowed. "You could bet all your money on that!"

Heidi started peeling off that pretty pink dress, and it was a race to see who could get naked the fastest.

They made love with sudden urgency the first time. Longarm mounted Heidi and drove his manhood in deep. Her body was as perfect as her face, and she was a tiger during their coupling, raking his back with her manicured fingernails, moaning and bucking under his weight and desire. When they were finally through, both Longarm and Heidi lay panting and staring up at the ceiling.

"You are very good," she said. "Arthur was quite controlled, and his . . . his willy was really very small."

"His *what*?"

Heidi jabbed him with her elbow in the ribs and blushed. "He called it his willy, and so I did too, but you probably have a different name for a penis, and yours, by the way, is awfully long and thick."

"Thank you," he said.

She rolled over on her side and looked down at his shrinking manhood. "And does your willy think that your willy will rise again before dinner . . . or after dinner?"

"Before," Longarm promised. "But my willy needs enough time to reload, and that is about as much time as it will take for you to refill our glasses and come back to bed."

"Very good!" Heidi jumped out of bed and strolled into the kitchen, her hips moving in a way that his willy was sure to take note of. When she returned, they sat on the bed for a while and talked.

"Did you know one of the things that I want most to do in America is to see the Grand Canyon?"

"Do tell."

"Yes," Heidi said, "I want very much to see it, and the idea of taking a boat ride through the canyon is wildly exciting."

Longarm heard alarm bells going off inside. "It's a dangerous thing to do and I'm hoping it won't be necessary."

"But all the same," Heidi said, "it's something that I'd dearly love to do, and the idea that we'd be trying to find bodies and solve a mysterious disappearance makes the whole thing all that much more exciting."

"Heidi," Longarm said, placing his glass down on a

bedside table. "That would be a bad idea. It's just too dangerous."

"I'm sure that I don't have to remind you that danger is the very spice of life."

"No," he said, "you don't have to remind me. But all the same, this is official business and there could be some real danger and hardship."

"I'm going with you," she told him. "This is a free country, and you really can't stop me, so why not make this easy and exciting for us both?"

"Heidi, please . . ."

But the woman wasn't listening. Instead, she was climbing onto his body and rubbing her bottom back and forth against his wee willy. Only it wasn't going to be wee for very long. And Longarm had the feeling that trying to stop Heidi Zalstra from doing what she wanted to do was an exercise in futility.

"It's hard again," she said. "And so very soon."

"Climb aboard!"

Heidi eased herself down on top of him in a sitting position, knees forward, and then she threw back her head and laughed and bounced. Bounced and surged until their bodies became as wild as the canyon and the river that awaited them in the Arizona Territory.

Chapter 3

Billy Vail came puffing up the loading platform. "Custis!" he called, waving his arms frantically.

Longarm leaned close to Heidi. "That's my boss, and he looks to be all lathered up about something."

"Maybe the pair of rich people have been found, and we won't be going to the Grand Canyon after all," Heidi Zalstra said.

"Maybe."

"Custis," Billy gasped, coming to a stop. "I'm glad I caught you before you boarded the train."

"We were just about to," Longarm replied.

"What do you mean, 'we'?" Billy asked, looking from Longarm to the beautiful woman at his side.

"Billy Vail, meet Heidi Zalstra, who also has a ticket for Arizona."

"Oh, no!" Billy said, still trying to catch his breath. "You can't go with him, Miss Zalstra."

"Why not? I'm originally from Holland, but as far as I know America is still a free country."

"It is!" Billy exclaimed. "But this trip is going to be

official business and very dangerous . . . not to mention hard."

"I like danger," Heidi told the man. "And your marshal has already tried to talk me out of going because of the hardships that we might face, but I decided it was the opportunity of a lifetime."

Billy looked to his big deputy marshal, eyes beseeching his help. "Custis?"

"Not a thing I can do about it," Longarm said with a shrug. "After all, this is a free country."

"But my god!" Billy exclaimed. "I've just received a telegram from Arizona that the bodies of three river guides at Lees Ferry were found dumped in the Colorado River, several miles below the crossing."

Longarm scowled. "Had they been shot?"

"Throats slit," Billy said nervously. Again, he looked to the beautiful lady standing close to Longarm. "Really, Miss Zalstra, it would be a terrible mistake to accompany my deputy to the Arizona Territory and specifically to Lees Ferry. Something very evil is taking place and no one knows what has happened to Mr. and Mrs. Quinn. For all we know, they've also had their throats cut and their bodies dumped in the river."

Heidi nodded, lips pursed in thought. After a moment and aware that both men were anxiously awaiting her decision, she said, "Marshal Vail, Custis has only good things to say about you, and so I do value your opinion . . . and well-intentioned advice. However, I just couldn't live with the idea of sitting around Denver waiting to hear if Custis either found the missing couple . . . or was murdered . . . or what!"

"But . . ."

"I have to go with him," she said. "And anyway, we've already bought two first-class tickets."

"You've bought 'first-class' tickets?"

"That's right," Longarm told his boss. "And we're going to travel in style comin' and goin' to the Grand Canyon."

"This is not supposed to be your vacation," Billy snapped with clear disapproval. "It's supposed to be a very dangerous assignment!"

"I know that and so does Heidi. But she assures me that she is an expert shot, and I might just need someone to watch my backside." He blushed. "And my other . . . uh . . . sides."

"Oh for gawd sakes!" Billy shouted. "I'm beginning to think that you've both completely lost your senses."

"That isn't all that I intend on losing once we get on that train," Longarm said, giving the beautiful blond woman a lascivious wink.

"Custis, you rogue!" Heidi giggled. "What fun we are going to have on that train."

"I've heard about as much as I can stomach," Billy snorted.

"Does that mean you've just decided to send someone else to that big ditch in the earth?" Longarm asked, raising an eyebrow. "'Cause if that's the case, I'm delighted."

"You wouldn't get all that I promised if you don't go," Billy warned.

"Oh," Longarm said, pulling out the piece of paper. "You mean the promise of a raise, promotion, and vacation?"

"That's right."

Heidi slipped her arm around Custis and laughed. "Actually, Marshal Vail, I've made Custis a much more attractive offer than you can possibly come up with or even imagine."

"I've a pretty good imagination about what you have offered," Billy said stiffly.

"That and much more," Heidi told him, a coolness in her voice. "I'm thinking about offering Custis a partnership."

"In what?" Longarm asked, as surprised as Billy.

"I haven't decided yet," she told them both. "And part of this journey we are about to undertake will tell me a good deal about Custis . . . his strengths . . . and weaknesses."

"I don't have any weaknesses," Longarm said.

"Oh, darling, we all have a few."

Billy had heard enough. "I can see that the news I've just delivered has had little or no influence on your decision to go as a pair. It's insane, of course, but as you said, Miss Zalstra, America is still a free country and so I can't stop you from going to Lees Ferry."

"Then don't waste your time in trying," she said sweetly.

Just then the locomotive blasted its shrill whistle. "The train is about to leave," Longarm said. "We'd better get to that special suite you reserved for us."

Billy shook his head. "A special suite? My gawd, Custis, you haven't even left Denver yet and I think that woman has already turned you to ruin."

"No, she hasn't," Longarm assured the small man. "Just have some faith in us, Billy. I'll get to the bottom of those murders and disappearances."

"Just make sure you and Miss Zalstra don't get to the bottom of the Colorado River," Billy warned as he bowed to Heidi and shook Longarm's hand.

"I'll see you in about three weeks . . . give or take one," Longarm told the man as he helped Heidi up onto the train's steps and then boarded as the car began to move.

Billy Vail stood at the depot until the train was just a

speck on the horizon. He was very worried and upset about the three corpses whose throats had been slashed and then dumped into the muddy river. He was even more worried about his best and favorite deputy, Custis Long.

"Sir?"

He turned to see a porter standing behind him. "Is there something wrong?"

"Why do you ask?"

The porter was a kid, really. Not more than twenty years old, with a cowlick and buckteeth. But he had a nice face and an honest and earnest appearance about him, and he was big, maybe six-foot-three and strong-looking.

"You ever think of becoming a lawman?" Billy asked, surprising even himself by the question.

"No."

"Well," Billy said, reaching into his pocket and giving the kid his business card. "If you ever do, why don't you get in contact with me at the federal building? I couldn't promise you a job, but I could make some inquiries in your behalf."

"Now, why in the world would you want to do that? You don't even know me, Marshal."

"I'm a good judge of people," Billy said, wishing he had never brought the subject up. "And you look to be someone who not only is concerned about others, but who takes a little initiative if something seems amiss."

"Well thank you! My name is Herman Pawalski and I do like people. But to tell you the truth, I also like staying alive."

Billy blinked.

"And I have talked to that big deputy marshal several times when he's comin' or goin' to some hellhole that you've sent him to. And I've seen him return to Denver shot up, cut up, and beat up."

Billy started to protest. "Now wait a darned minute, Herman!"

"No, sir," the kid said, "you wait a minute. I ain't ever goin' to be famous or rich . . . but I intend to live a full life and end up in one piece when I resign myself to a rocking chair on some porch with some old lady by my side. Railroad has promised that I'm going to be a conductor someday if I keep my nose clean . . . but I'd rather be the engineer that runs the show."

"That's fine," Billy snapped. "I'm sorry I even mentioned a career as a law officer."

"Aw, you was just trying to be friendly and . . . if I hadn't seen your big deputy marshal so shot up, cut up, and beat up so often . . . well, I might have taken your bait."

"Give me back my damned card," Billy growled.

Herman Pawalski gave the card back, offered his bucktoothed grin, and headed off down the line.

Chapter 4

"Flagstaff! Flagstaff! Next stop is Flagstaff, Arizona Territory!" the conductor of their Atchison, Topeka & Santa Fe train called as he worked his way through the passenger cars.

Longarm was making love once more to Heidi, savoring the rocking motion of their first-class passenger car and luxurious accommodations. Heidi was on her hands and knees, head down and grinning at the sight between her thighs. "Come on, darling, we're supposed to be getting off this train in a few minutes!"

"Don't rush me," he grunted, tightening his grip on her hips and slamming his manhood in and out faster and faster.

"Flagstaff! You folks in there ready to—Oh, my gawd! I'm sorry to . . ."

"Get out of here!" Longarm growled as the conductor turned crimson with embarrassment and shut the door to their compartment.

"Oh, dear," Heidi fretted. "We forgot to lock the door again!"

"Well, maybe he learned something."

"I doubt it," Heidi grunted. "Oh, that feels so . . . delicious!"

"Don't it though?" Longarm came to his climax and Heidi moaned with pleasure. Moments later, she was on top of him and riding his rod hard. "Oh, I'm going to miss this so much!"

"Me too! But just because we're getting off the train doesn't—"

Heidi cried out in ecstasy and then collapsed on top of Longarm, both of them sweaty and panting just as the train pulled into the station.

Longarm and Heidi wiped the sweat and sex off themselves and quickly dressed. They were climbing down from the train in less than five minutes, and their conductor was nowhere in sight.

"We must have shocked him pretty badly," Heidi said, looking concerned. "I wanted to give the poor man a generous tip."

"We'll give it to him on the return run," Longarm said, "if he has gotten over his embarrassment and can look either one of us in the eye."

"Poor man! I feel badly about that."

"Yeah, me too," Longarm said, obviously not meaning it. "There are our bags."

Heidi had four pieces of luggage, all of them sizable. Longarm was accustomed to traveling light and had only his one large leather valise with change of underclothing, shirt, and a few other personal things. In addition, he carried his own Winchester, a Colt Model T. caliber .44-40, and, attached to his watch fob, a twin-barreled .44-caliber derringer. The derringer was used only as a last resort, and it had saved his bacon on more than one occasion.

A young man hurried up to them. "Need some help with those bags and a ride to a hotel?"

"Sure do," Longarm said. "How much?"

"A dollar," the man said. "Got a nice buggy waiting close by, and I'll carry your bags right up to the registration desk and not drop 'em off in front like some do."

"You're hired," Heidi said. "And you are worth two dollars to us."

"Thank you very much!" the man said, swallowing hard and trying not to stare at Heidi. "Very generous of you, ma'am!"

"Hotel Weatherford."

"Very good, sir!"

"Is that the finest hotel in Flagstaff?" Heidi asked, looking around at her surroundings and looking somewhat disappointed because the town was small, dirty, and raw compared to the far more metropolitan Denver.

"It's nicer than what I usually stay at when I'm in Flagstaff."

"It's a very fine hotel," the young man said, grabbing up all the bags except the one that Longarm was carrying. "The food in their dining room is as good as you'll find anywhere in town."

"What do you like personally?" Heidi asked.

"Huh?"

"Your personal recommendation concerning the hotel's menu?"

"Uh . . . well, ma'am, I've never actually eaten there myself. A bit too expensive for me. But I've heard they serve a fine steak and also that they offer a varied menu and even serve up roasted pheasant!"

"That does sound delicious," Heidi told him. "And here, a little extra for your good recommendation."

"*Five* dollars?" he asked, staring at the money she had placed in his calloused hand. "Why, thank you!"

"You are quite welcome," Heidi said. "Now, if we could get moving, I am anxious for a bath and a nice clean and quiet place to piddle."

The man blushed and hobbled off with her four large pieces of luggage. Longarm was impressed with the kid and grinning as he followed him and Heidi to a buggy.

"Piddle?" he chuckled with a grin on his handsome face.

The Hotel Weatherford was right up the street from the train station, on Leroux Street in the middle of town. It was a big, multistoried brick building that stood proudly over its shorter neighbors; the registration desk was walnut and the lobby quite elegant.

"A suite," Heidi said to the clerk. "Something with a view other than a back alley."

"Of course, Mrs. . . . ?"

"Mrs. Long?" she asked, looking up at Custis.

"Sure, that'll work."

The registration clerk gave them a strange and confused look, but he wrote down the particulars. "May I ask how long you'll be staying as our guests?"

"Only tonight and maybe tomorrow night. We need to get up to the Colorado River and the Grand Canyon."

"I see. There is a stagecoach that will take you up there, and it leaves this coming Wednesday."

"That's four days from now, and we haven't got that much time to waste," Custis said.

"We could hire a private coach," Heidi quietly suggested.

"Or horses."

"I would prefer our own private coach."

"Fair enough. A coach it is." Longarm turned back to the clerk. "Can you tell me where I can hire one?"

The clerk gave him the names of two men who had liveries and who might be able to take them north. "But it will be expensive. It's quite a trip up to the Grand Canyon and Lees Ferry."

"How far would you reckon?" Longarm asked.

"Well over a hundred difficult miles. I'd say closer to one hundred and forty miles of hard road."

"Oh, dear, that far!" Heidi said.

"I'm afraid so, Mrs. Long. And you might want to reconsider the idea of going up there. The canyon is just a big ditch in the dirt, and I'm told the Colorado River isn't anything to brag about. It's muddy and dangerous. Maybe you'd rather see our Painted Desert or Petrified Forest. They're a good sight closer to Flagstaff, and that's what most of our guests come to see. Really beautiful sight, and those big trees that have turned to stone are something that you'll never forget. Why, you can buy or even pick up pieces of petrified wood all over the place. Most of us around here have a ton of the stuff. It's really beautiful when you get it wet and you can see the tree rings, the bark, and everything!"

"Well, that does sound fascinating," Heidi said, "but we really must get up to Lees Ferry. Custis . . . I mean Marshal Custis Long . . . is a federal marshal, and we've come to investigate the terrible murders that have taken place up by Lees Ferry."

The clerk stared at Longarm. "You're a lawman with . . ."

"With her?" Longarm asked, brow furrowed. "That's right. But I'd prefer that you keep that piece of information to yourself. In fact, I *insist* on it."

"Yes, sir! I mean, yes, sir, Marshal Long! My lips are glued."

"If they aren't, I'll come back from Lees Ferry and sew them together with horsehair."

The clerk paled and dipped his chin up and down rapidly.

When they were in their suite, Heidi turned on Longarm and said, "You really didn't need to put such a fright into that clerk downstairs."

"Oh, but I did," Longarm countered. "And while we are on this subject, I need to say that I never let anyone know I'm a federal officer of the law."

"And why not?"

"Because there are plenty of men that just hate law officers and some that would love nothing more than to put a bullet in my back."

"Oh, I see."

"I hope you do, Heidi. I really hope you try and remember that, because it will make my job easier and a damn sight safer."

"I'll remember." She smiled. "Now, if you'll excuse me, I really do have to piddle!"

"Chamber pot is usually under the bed, or there may be a running toilet at the end of the hall in a place this fancy."

"You've never stayed here either?"

"Nope. Like the fella at the train station, the Hotel Weatherford has always been a little rich for my wallet."

"Not this trip it isn't," she said, blowing him a kiss and stooping to peer under their bed.

"Find it?"

She dragged out a porcelain chamber pot that was decorated with purple pansies. "How cute."

"Use it," he said, heading for the door to find them a bottle of whiskey and another of good chardonnay wine.

Chapter 5

Longarm visited a livery that looked prosperous, and when he found the owner, a large man who smelled like a pile of ripe horse turds, and told the man that he wanted to rent a private coach, the liveryman laughed.

"I sure as hell won't help you."

Longarm frowned. "Mind telling me why not?"

"Because there is a stage that goes up to Lees Ferry and I can't compete with them."

"We're in a hurry."

"Yeah," the man said, "I'll just bet you are."

"What's that supposed to mean?"

"I *know* who you are, Marshal. And I'm not stupid. You're in a hurry to get up there so you can investigate the murders and that missing judge and his young wife."

"I guess you got me pegged," Longarm said.

"There's another thing, and that is that I don't like anyone who wears a badge . . . especially a federal badge."

"Fair enough," Longarm said, turning on his heel and starting to leave.

"Hey, don't you turn your back on me before I'm through talking!"

Longarm turned.

"Do you remember a man named Reece Whitfield?" the liveryman said with a snarl in his voice.

"Yeah, I shot the asshole dead about three years ago right here in Flagstaff."

"Reece was my kid brother."

"Come to think of it, I do remember that fat bastard smelled almost as bad as yourself."

"You son of a bitch, you just *insulted* my dear dead brother!"

"I guess I did," Longarm conceded. "Truth is, I'm starting to remember you now. You got away with a bank robbery while your brother took the blame for it and I hunted him down. Like you, he was stupid and thought he was a real bad fella, so he tried to pull a gun on me and I drilled him twice before he could even get the pistol out of his holster."

The big liveryman's mouth twisted down at the corners. "My brother would be alive now if it wasn't for *you!*"

"I'm surprised," Longarm said, "that someone in Flagstaff hasn't shot you down."

"No one has the balls to try."

Longarm was wearing his sidearm, and he noted that this angry man had inched closer to a double-barreled shotgun that was leaning up against a wall. "Mister," he said, "I can tell that you are nearly feeble-minded, and I can read your mind like a cheap dime novel, and I can tell you right now that you'll be dead before you can pick that scattergun up."

The liveryman glanced at the shotgun, which was almost within arm's reach. "I guess you probably could at that," he said. "But I'm a patient man. I can wait for my time."

"If that's a threat, I won't give you the time to wait."

The liveryman raised his hands up near his shoulders. "You gonna gun me down? You gonna arrest me?"

"I'm considering it."

The man grinned wickedly. "Sheriff Clyde Petrie is my cousin. You arrest me and take me to jail, then you'll look like a fool. Clyde will laugh in your face and so will I."

Longarm expected this was true. In his long time as a federal marshal, he'd often come up against local law officers who not only envied him for his much higher pay, but also considered him a rival. Local law officers resented any higher authority that entered their jurisdiction.

"It's a long way up to Lees Ferry and the Grand Canyon," the liveryman crowed.

"So I've been told. What's your name?"

"Carl Whitfield."

"Well, Carl, I can see that you and I are just not going to be doing business. And I've got a piece of advice that you ought to pay attention to."

Carl hawked and spat a stream of brown tobacco juice between them. "Marshal, I sure as hell don't want any of your damned advice."

"Take it anyway," Longarm said. "If you so much as cross my path, local law or not, I'll put a bullet hole in you before you can bat an eye, and I'll walk up and laugh in your pig face."

Whitfield swallowed and spat again, all his teeth stained brown. "I'll keep that in mind when we meet somewhere on the trail."

"Does that mean that you're going to try to ambush me on the way up to Lees Ferry?"

A craftiness crept into the man's close-set eyes. "I didn't say that."

"Yeah, but that was your message."

Whitfield paused and took a deep breath. "There's a man named Clayton that lives just up the street. If the price is right, Otis Clayton will take you north in a wagon or he'll rent you horses for the trip. If I were you, Marshal, I'd go see Otis and tell him I sent you his way. He'll take care of you."

"Is that right?"

"For a fact," Whitfield said, smiling coldly.

"Is this fella named Otis Clayton by any chance related to you or the town marshal?"

Whitfield rubbed the stubble of his jowls. "Might be."

Longarm shook his head. "Carl, my only regret here is that you didn't make a grab for the shotgun. I'm sure that I'll have the opportunity to kill you sooner rather than later."

"I hear you have a yellow-haired beauty traveling with you," Whitfield said. "She your whore?"

Longarm had been willing to put off this confrontation until another time. But because of this crude insult to Heidi, he decided that he just couldn't wait until later.

Reversing his direction, Longarm reached across his belt and unholstered his Colt as he kept walking forward. Whitfield's nasty grin dissolved and his eyes widened with fear. "Now, wait just a damned—"

Longarm didn't give the man a chance to say another word as he slashed the barrel of his big Colt across Whitfield's face, opening up a deep gash. Blood cascaded down the liveryman's ugly face, and he staggered backward. Longarm went after him with fists and boots. He caught Whitfield with a wicked kick to the groin that caused the man to scream. When Whitfield's dirty mouth flew open in a howl, Longarm closed that mouth with a tremendous uppercut to the jaw that sent the big man backpedaling into the side of his barn. Longarm hammered Whitfield across the bridge of his nose and heard bone crunch. The liveryman collapsed on his knees, trying to cover his destroyed face.

Longarm stepped back and holstered his weapon. "You may own a livery, but you're still the same piece of rotten trash as your kid brother. Next time we meet, I'll kill you and think up a legitimate reason afterward. Is that crystal clear, you stinking piece of horse shit?"

Whitfield moaned, face a mask of blood.

"I'll take that as a yes," Longarm said to the beaten man before walking away.

He did not go to see Otis Clayton but instead found the local stage station, where he met the owner, whose name was John Wallace. Wallace was middle-aged and of average size. He had a band of hair around his ears, but the top of his head was bald as a billiard ball and shiny. But what Longarm liked about Wallace was that the man looked him straight in the eyes when they talked, and he was no bragger.

"I operate a stagecoach to and from the Grand Canyon once a week."

"It doesn't leave until Wednesday and we can't wait that long."

"That's only four days off. If I were you, I'd reserve a seat, and between now and then I'd visit—"

Longarm cut the man off but not in an offensive way. "I'm a deputy United States marshal from Denver and I have to get up to Lees Ferry right away on an investigation."

"Oh."

"Can you help me and my partner?"

"They sent *two* U.S. marshals all the way from Denver?"

"No," Longarm said, knowing what he was about to say would sound foolish. "I'm traveling with my . . . uh, wife."

Wallace hid his thoughts well. "Marshal, it's none of my business, but I sure don't understand why a man would take his wife up there to the Colorado River and that big old canyon. From what I understand, two men just had their throats cut and—"

"Listen," Longarm said. "My situation is complicated."

"I'd say that."

"But here's the thing, John. We need to go and we need to go tomorrow. Is there any way that you can help us?"

"I can't take you up in the stagecoach because I already have passengers booked for next Wednesday. Some of them have money and have come a long, long way to visit the Grand Canyon. But what I can do is rent you a couple of good saddle horses and even a reliable pack animal . . . horse or burro. You'd have to provision yourself for the journey, of course, but you'd make good time once you were on the road."

"If that's the best that can be done, then we'll do it," Longarm decided, knowing that Heidi would not be pleased. He didn't even know if she was able to ride a horse . . . especially for over a hundred miles. But she'd either do it or have to wait and take next Wednesday's stagecoach, which might be the best thing anyway.

"I can show you a pair of animals that I think will serve you and your wife well. But I'll warn you right up front," Wallace said, "this is going to cost you a helluva lot of money."

"How much?" Longarm asked, knowing that Heidi would foot the bill . . . unless she changed her mind and decided not to go north.

"How about a hundred and fifty dollars?"

"That sounds *way* too high."

"One hundred for the rental and fifty for a deposit that you can have back on my good horses, a pack burro, and the saddles and outfit you'll need. Oh, and I'll throw in forty pounds of oats."

Longarm knew that he had few other choices other than to wait for the regularly scheduled stagecoach run. "Fair enough . . . if I like the animals."

"You'll like them," Wallace promised. "What you won't like is the travel north. It's tough and dangerous country. I won't try to hide it . . . there are thieves and worse out there, and some of them are desperate enough to kill a man. I don't even want to speak about what they would do to a pretty woman."

"How do you know she's 'pretty'?"

John Wallace grinned. "Hell, this is still a small town. Don't you imagine that when you two got off the train every man in town heard about how beautiful your companion was even before you got to the hotel?"

"I never gave the matter much thought," Longarm confessed.

"Well, not only does everyone know that she's a blond beauty, they are of the opinion that she isn't really your wife."

"Why would they decide that?"

"Because rich and beautiful women aren't in the habit of marrying poor workingmen like ourselves."

Longarm had to smile. "Seems like the people in Flagstaff don't have much to do but gossip about other men's business."

Wallace grinned. "Like I said, it's still a small town."

"Let's take a look at those animals you want to make your fortune on."

"They're right out in the back," Wallace said. "And by the way, I remember you killed Reece Whitfield and done the town a big favor."

"I might also have to kill his brother Carl."

"That would be another huge favor. The man gets drunk and beats up on smaller folks. He's full of anger and he'll cheat anyone that doesn't yet know him well."

"Carl isn't going to do much of anything for a few days."

"Oh, and why is that?" Wallace asked.

"Because he's not feeling well since we met up a short while ago."

Wallace stared, but Longarm wasn't in the mood to satisfy the man's curiosity, so he headed out the door to see what kind of horses and pack animals the man had in mind to rent.

Chapter 6

Longarm went back to the Hotel Weatherford, and when he entered the room, Heidi was reading a local newspaper while a Chinaman was filling a huge tub with buckets of steamy water.

"You got a bathtub moved in here?" Longarm asked.

"Sure. I thought you'd like one, and I've ordered some food and drinks to be brought up at five."

"Must be nice to have money."

"It is. Why don't you start thinking about the proposition that I made you before we left Denver?"

"You mean the one about handing in my badge?"

"Yes, that one."

Longarm removed his coat and hat and waited for the Chinaman to finish filling the tub. When the man was done, he bowed and Heidi gave him a few dollars, which pleased the Chinaman very much.

"He's a nice little fellow," Heidi said when they were alone. "He can't speak a word of English, but he's smart as anything and it was easy enough to let him know what I needed."

"That's good."

She put down her paper and smiled. "So, when are we leaving tomorrow morning on the stagecoach?"

"Well, we're not," he said, deciding to get right to the point. "I couldn't find a buggy or coach, so I rented us a couple of horses and a pack burro."

"What!" She dropped her newspaper and stared at him. "Are you crazy! The clerk down at the registration desk said that it was over a hundred miles up to the Grand Canyon."

"More like a hundred and forty."

"I can't ride that far!"

"Have you ever ridden a horse?"

"No, and I'm not going to start tomorrow morning."

Longarm took a chair. "Listen," he said. "I've got to leave in the morning, and I can't wait around for the stagecoach, but . . . *you* can."

"You're suggesting that I wait here and take the coach while you ride out by yourself?"

"That's exactly what I'm suggesting," Longarm told her. "There is no point in you suffering saddle sores, blisters, and all the hardships of the trail. I'll go on, and you follow on the stagecoach. That way, we'll both be happier."

Heidi's lips turned down at the corners. "I don't like this very much."

"I know you don't," Longarm told her, "but think hard about it. You've never ridden before, and you would be miserable riding a horse that many miles. The insides of those lovely thighs would become blistered, and the blisters would burn like fire and weep. Is that what you want?"

"Of course not."

"Then do as I suggest and wait here in the lap of

luxury and come on the stage. I've made arrangements for two horses, but that can be changed in the morning, and I'll tell him to hold a seat on Wednesday's stagecoach for you."

Heidi got up and came to sit in Longarm's lap. She kissed his face and whispered, "I don't want you to leave me."

"I can travel a lot faster alone," he said frankly. "And you'd suffer too much on horseback."

"But what if something terrible happens to you before I get to this place called Lees Ferry?"

"Better something terrible happens to just me rather than us both, if it came to that. And if it does, I'd want you safe. I'd want you to take care of . . . of things if I couldn't."

Tears welled up in her eyes. "This kind of talk upsets me, Custis."

"I'll be fine and so will you. The stage line's owner is named John Wallace, and he's a good, solid man. He'll see that you're kept safe and that you reach me by Friday or Saturday."

"I'll have to ride in a stagecoach for two or three days?"

"It will be an adventure," Longarm told her. "Remember how you told me that you love adventures?"

"Yes, but not alone."

"You won't be alone," he told her. "There will be other passengers on the stagecoach. You'll probably meet some nice and interesting people."

"I doubt that."

"Heidi, try to be reasonable. This is the best way."

"Custis," she whispered, "my heart tells me to get on a horse and ride a hundred and forty miles . . . but my head says otherwise."

"I want those lovely silken thighs to stay lovely and silken," he told her as he slipped his hand between her legs and kissed her lips.

"All right," she finally agreed. "I'll wait. But what am I supposed to do for the next three days in this lumber town?"

"You'll think of something."

She wasn't pleased, but she was resigned. "Let's get into the bathtub while it's still hot."

"I'd like that," he said. "Nice things can happen when a man and a woman get in a bathtub."

"You'd probably drown me if you got excited."

"You could be on top," he said, chuckling.

"Then I might drown *you*!"

Longarm scooted her off his lap and began to undress. He figured that this bath was going to be just the thing to take their mind off the difficult days that most surely awaited them both.

"When are the drinks coming up to our room?"

"Any minute now."

"Then maybe we ought to wait a few minutes so we don't shock the nice Chinaman like we did that poor fella on the train when he stuck his head into our compartment."

Heidi, remembering, burst into wild laughter and started undressing anyway.

Chapter 7

Longarm left their hotel room early the next morning while Heidi was still sleeping. He had a slight hangover and was tired from lack of sleep, but he figured that a good breakfast, a few cups of strong coffee, and he'd be up to snuff again. He had his rifle and personals and was ready to get started on his journey up to Lees Ferry.

The Pine Cone Café was just opening when Longarm entered, and he finished a hearty breakfast as the sun came up over the eastern horizon. By seven, he had gone to the livery to meet John Wallace.

"My wife won't be coming along on horseback," he explained. "She's never really ridden before, and I convinced her to take your stagecoach up to the Grand Canyon along with your other passengers."

"That's probably a smart idea," the liveryman grudgingly admitted, "but I would have made more money if you'd have rented two horses."

"How many passengers have you got booked on the stagecoach coming up on Wednesday?"

"Three, and now your wife makes four." Wallace smiled. "There are always a couple more that buy tickets at the last minute, and a full coach is six."

"Save a seat for my wife, who will be by today or tomorrow for her ticket," Longarm told the man as they went to get the horses.

"The truth is," Wallace said, "if the word got out that a man could sit close to your lovely wife for three days in a stagecoach, I'd have a line of ticket takers stretching out into the street."

Longarm chuckled. "Heidi is a looker, all right."

"Prettiest woman I've seen in years," the liveryman said, "maybe ever."

Longarm couldn't argue the point.

"You sure are a lucky man to have a wife that beautiful."

Longarm felt guilty about the deception, but he and Heidi had just decided it would be easier all the way around for them both if people thought they were married. So he nodded and said, "Let's get the horses saddled. I want to get a good start on the day."

"It's going to be warm," Wallace told him. "But not too hot. You should make good time."

"Think I can be up to Lees Ferry by tomorrow night?"

"You might be able to do that, but you'd have to really put the move on."

"Tell you what," Longarm said. "How about I forget the pack animal and just take one fast horse? I can probably buy any supplies along the way that I can't stuff into a saddlebag."

John Wallace shook his head. "Every time you open your mouth I'm losin' more money."

"Sorry about that," Longarm told him. "But just

remember that you're going to sell out every seat on your stagecoach after my wife buys a ticket."

"Yeah, there is that, I reckon."

Thirty minutes later, Longarm was in the saddle and galloping north out of Flagstaff. He reckoned it was still before nine o'clock, and the horse that he and Wallace had decided was best was a fine-looking buckskin mare. She had long legs and a pretty black tail and mane.

"Her name is Sassy and she's the best horse I own," Wallace had told him. "If you lame her or lose her, it'll cost you an even hundred dollars."

"I don't intend to do either. I'll push the mare, but I won't ruin good horseflesh."

"I knew you'd promise me that. Otherwise, I'd have given you a far lesser animal."

Now, with the mare set at a steady jog that would carry him farther and faster, Longarm climbed over a high rise and then rode down toward the vast Coconino Plateau country. By midday he'd reached what was called the Little Grand Canyon but was in fact a mostly dry canyon, where an old Navajo trading post stood on the edge of the south cliff. The trading post looked to be prosperous, and there were quite a few Indian ponies and supply wagons tied in front of the post.

Longarm dismounted and tied the buckskin mare off a ways by herself. He knew that the locals would take note of Sassy's exceptional looks, and he was a little worried that some young Navajo just might untie the mare, leap into the saddle, and ride like hell for parts unknown.

Still, he had a need to buy a few basic supplies along with cigars and a box of ammunition for his rifle . . .

maybe a warm Navajo blanket in case the nights got chilly and some jerky and coffee.

When he entered the trading post, all conversation stopped. The room was filled with Navajo families; cute little kids with big black eyes and women who wore long and colorful velvet skirts and turquoise and silver jewelry.

Longarm nodded to everyone and they finally nodded back. Like most Indian trading posts he'd visited, this one was packed with all sorts of interesting goods. Mostly it had big rolls of sheep wool and pelts along with barrels of pickles, crackers, and pigs' feet.

"Howdy," a white man said in greeting, from behind the glass counter filled with silver and turquoise. "What can I get for you today?"

Longarm gave the clerk his short order. "I carry everything you need, but I'm sorry that I can't sell you any whiskey on the reservation."

"I didn't ask to buy any," Longarm replied. "But I could use some chili peppers and two pounds of salted pork along with the other things I've already mentioned."

"Won't take but a few minutes to fill your order. In the meantime, you can mosey around and see if there's anything else that catches your eye."

"Oh, there are probably plenty of things that I'd like to buy . . . but I'm on a tight budget."

"We've got some real fine Navajo jewelry on sale," the clerk told him, tapping the top of the glass and looking down at the assortment of jewelry. "I've been told that Navajo jewelry brings quite a price back east."

"I'm from Denver and I don't need any jewelry."

"Suit yourself," the clerk said with a curt smile as he hurried off to fill the order.

For the next twenty minutes, Longarm wandered

around in the trading post looking at the amazing variety of goods. Horseshoes, bows and arrows, old cap-and-ball pistols, knives with beautiful handles of silver inlay and blades long enough to qualify as sabers, foods that looked as though they might be highly toxic to a white man's stomach, and leather goods—shirts, moccasins, and many other items, all intricately beaded in many designs— rocks with crystals and turquoise in them, petrified wood, even seashell necklaces. But it was the withered mummy in a pine coffin with a glass top that really caught Long-arm's full attention.

The mummy was small, perhaps only five feet long, and his skin stretched over his prominent facial and skel-etal bones like old parchment paper. His hair was black and adorned with two eagle feathers, giving Custis the impression that the ancient Indian had died young. There was a death grin on his thin lips, and most of the mum-my's teeth were missing. He wore a faded old animal skin, but someone had obviously slipped a few turquoise rings on his bony fingers and a silver bracelet on his left wrist to dress up his appearance.

Longarm stared at the mummy for several minutes. So this was what a body looked like after it had lain untouched in some arid and ancient cliff dwelling for hundreds and hundreds of years.

"His name is Indian Joe," the clerk said, coming up behind Longarm. "I call all the ones that look like war-riors Indian Joe."

"Where did he come from?"

"Beats the hell out of me. Could be anywhere around here or up in Colorado. People . . . mostly white prospec-tors and trappers . . . bring them in here to sell or trade. I don't like to keep more than a few of 'em on display at the same time."

Longarm couldn't hide his astonishment. "People actually *buy* these things?"

"Oh, yes!" The clerk snapped his suspenders. "And you won't believe the price they pay."

"How much for this poor Indian Joe?" Longarm had to ask out of curiosity.

"Two hundred and fifty dollars, which includes the jewelry, his clothes, and the pine box . . . but not any money for transporting him down to Flagstaff to be put on a train."

Longarm whistled. "Why on earth would anyone pay that kind of money for a mummy?"

"Because if they can get Indian Joe back to the East Coast museums of natural history, he will easily bring a thousand dollars. Trouble is . . . and I tell all my buyers this right up front . . . these mummies are *extremely* fragile. You bump one and an arm might fall off, or the foot. I've heard that some of these mummies have arrived by train in places like Boston or New York looking like piles of dust and leather. Of course, then they are worthless except for the value of the skulls."

"Of course." Longarm shook his head. "I'd have thought that the local Navajo might have taken exception to their ancestors being carted off to some museum."

"Oh, some of them do . . . some don't. It's really about the money. To keep down the objections from the locals, I do promise them twenty percent of every dollar I make selling their mummified ancestors."

"That's real white of you, mister." Longarm had seen enough of the mummy for one lifetime and marched back to the counter, where his supplies were bagged and waiting.

"Be five dollars and eighty-six cents. I saw you are

riding a fine buckskin. How about a few pounds of oats and maybe even some sugar cubes for the animal?"

Longarm had forgotten to get oats from John Wallace. "That would be a good idea."

"Horse need shoein'?" the man asked. "We do that for six dollars."

"That's pretty high, isn't it?"

"Not for a good job. If you're taking the road up to the Grand Canyon, you'll find it's damned rocky. Indian ponies, of course, have feet like iron and they get by . . . but a fine buckskin like that could go lame if she is unshod or even poorly shod."

"She's okay," Longarm said, picking up his packages and heading for the door.

"Come back again! I'll most likely have a better selection of mummies next time." He laughed and then he winked. "Maybe even a girl or two."

Longarm was so disgusted by the idea of stealing bodies and selling them off as curiosity pieces that he didn't even reply.

When he left the trading post, two Navajo dressed in denim work shirts, buckskin breeches, and moccasins were studying the mare from every angle.

"Hello," Longarm said, approaching the pair. "Nice day."

The larger and younger of the two pointed to the mare and grunted. "Sell for ten dollars."

"No, thanks."

The Indians went into a serious conversation in the Navajo language while Longarm stuffed his new purchases into his saddlebags and then untied the buckskin and prepared to mount up and ride away.

But the older of the Navajo grabbed the mare's reins

and held her still for a moment, grunting, "Thirteen dollars and a good wool blanket."

"No, thanks." Longarm smiled. "Now you need to let go of my horse's reins because I'm riding on."

The pair stepped back, and the younger one said, "Twenty dollars. No more."

"Not for sale."

The Indians shook their heads and looked at Longarm as if he was crazy, then they turned and went into the trading post, heads down and looking dejected.

"You ought to thank me for not selling you," Longarm told the mare as he used a winding and well-used trail that led down into the deep and wide gorge. "From the looks of the Navajo Indian ponies I've seen on this reservation, you'd have pretty much had to live off the land and fend for yourself."

The mare tossed her pretty head and moved smartly toward the trail that led down into the Little Colorado Gorge.

Chapter 8

Carl Whitfield and his cousin Al Hunt were lying flat on the red earth, and each had a pair of binoculars glued to their faces.

"He's coming up the north side of the Little Colorado Gorge," Hunt said. "I didn't think he'd take the long way around this gorge like the wagons. We could kill him when he crests the top."

But Whitfield shook his head. "Might be someone over at the trading post watching him until he passes over the rim and rides north a few miles. We'll take him up in the hills."

"Got to be careful not to let him see our tracks."

"We'll stay a mile west of him. I know a place that the road passes through a cut in the hills and it'll be perfect for an ambush."

"Hope it isn't too far," Hunt whined. "I'd like to get back to Flagstaff by tonight."

"Might not be possible. We have to bury that federal marshal so deep that he'll never be found."

"If we're going to do that, then why didn't we bring a pick and a shovel?"

Whitfield curbed his anger. "Because I forgot. I had a lot on my mind before we left town."

"Yeah," Hunt said, unable to conceal a smirk. "And from the looks of your face, I'd say maybe the marshal rearranged some of your brain."

"Shut up! We'll just have to find a low place maybe in some arroyo and cover him with dirt and rocks even if we do it with our bare hands."

"To hell with that plan. I say we just drag his body out in those dry hills and let the coyotes and vultures do the rest of the work. And what about that buckskin mare he's riding?"

Carl Whitfield had been thinking a lot about the mare. "She's too good to shoot, but we dare not take her back to Flagstaff, because everyone there knows the buckskin belongs to John Wallace. If we showed up with that animal, we'd be puttin' a noose around our necks."

"I guess that's true," Al agreed, "but it seems mighty sad to just drop a fine horse like that. Hey, maybe we should sell her at that trading post."

Whitfield thought about that for several minutes. "Too risky. People will remember that horse and its rider. What are we gonna tell 'em when we show up with the buckskin? That the rider fell off and broke his fool neck not long after he left the post?"

"Sounds good to me."

"Well," Whitfield groused, "it wouldn't wash! But we could take the mare and the saddle over to the Hopi Reservation. I hear that there's a big trading post at a place called Keams Canyon."

"How far out of our way would that be?"

"Fifty, maybe sixty miles. An extra two days at most."

"You think the mare is worth it?"

Whitfield nodded. "I sure as hell do. I'm certain we can get seventy or eighty dollars for her. Maybe even stir up a race. Those Hopi love betting on horse races, and I've seen the buckskin mare run before and she's damn near unbeatable."

"We got any money to put up on her?"

"I got thirty dollars cash. How much do you have?" Whitfield asked.

"Maybe twelve dollars."

"That's not a lot," Whitfield said. "But we could put up our own horses and saddles as part of the betting."

"And if we lost the race, what the hell would happen to us?" Hunt snapped. "We'd be up shit creek with no paddle. You reckon we could walk all the way back to Flagstaff?"

Whitfield shook his head. "Your problem is that you always worry too damn much about everything and are afraid to take a risk. I'm telling you, that buckskin mare is the fastest thing on four legs for a thousand damn miles. And you weigh no more than one hundred forty pounds soaking wet, so you could ride the mare. Al, for a little extra work and time, we can come out of this with five or six hundred dollars!"

"And kill the federal marshal."

"That's right," Whitfield said, rubbing a hand over his battered and swollen face. "And there's even more."

"Keep talkin'."

"The marshal's wife is going to be going up to Lees Ferry . . . *alone.*"

"But she'll be on the stagecoach."

"Not all the time," Whitfield said. "The stage holds over one night to rest the horses and passengers. We might be able to snatch her there."

Hunt broke into a big smile. "And have our dirty ways with her before we kill her?"

"Yep. Or else figure out a way to ransom the beautiful bitch. It's clear that she's loaded with money. What's to lose?"

Al Hunt chuckled obscenely. "I seen her when she got off the train and went into the hotel. Best-looking woman I've laid eyes on in years. Sure would like to ride her to a standstill."

"Me too," Whitfield said, voice hoarse with desire. "At the very worst, we could screw her for a few days and take all that jewelry she wears. I wouldn't doubt that she's also carrying plenty of cash."

Hunt sleeved sweat from his bloodshot eyes. Up here on the Navajo reservation the dirt was red and fine, and there was alkali mixed in as well, and that was painful to the eyes. "Let's get on our horses and get up ahead to that ambush place you were talking about."

Whitefield thought that was a fine idea. He desperately wanted to kill the federal marshal who had once shot his brother to death. He'd wanted to kill the marshal in Flagstaff, even more after the bastard beat him up, and now his need for revenge was almost at a fever pitch.

Once they were on their horses, they kept the low, sage-covered hills between themselves and the federal marshal and made sure that they didn't push their mounts hard enough to raise a dust trail.

"You know something," Al said, "I got me a hard one just thinking about that blond woman and how much fun we're going to have riding her while she hollers for mercy. I want her first, Carl. I *got* to have her first."

"We'll flip a coin for that," Carl Whitfield said, feeling his own manhood swelling at the thought of the pleasure they'd be taking from the rich woman in just another day. "'Cause I want her real bad, too."

Al Hunt gave his cousin a hard look, which the livery-man didn't even notice, but Al saw that there was a twisted smile on his blood-crusted lips.

Two hours later, Whitfield suddenly raised an arm and pointed to a gap in the hills just a mile ahead. "That's the place."

Hunt pulled his hat brim low and squinted into the dry, colorless distance. "You sure?"

"I'm dead sure. We'll ride around to the north and take our shooting positions on both sides of the gap. When the marshal comes through, he'll be in both our rifle sights, and it'll be like a shooting gallery. Thing to remember is, don't shoot too high and risk hitting each other and we damn sure don't want to accidentally put a bullet in the mare."

"I'm a better shot than you are," Al Hunt said. "I'll take the first shot, and if he's still alive, you open fire."

"Fair enough," Whitfield agreed. "But we can't let the mare race off, because sure as hell she'll run all the way back to the Flagstaff and that stable where she's been kept for years."

"She'd run that far on her own?"

"Maybe," Whitfield said, hedging. "But we just can't take the chance on it. She'll be spooked and might even be covered with the marshal's blood. We've got to make sure we catch her up, even if she'd only run as far south as the trading post."

"I don't see that as being a problem," Hunt snapped.

"Well, I do," Whitfield argued. "Because I've seen the mare run and I know she's a hell of a lot faster than the horses carrying our carcasses."

"And you said *I* was a big worrier," Hunt drawled. "Well look who is the worrier now."

Carl Whitfield had never really liked this cousin, but he knew the man had killed before and wouldn't hesitate to do it again in order to make some big money. Add that to the fact that Al was already salivating over the thought of repeatedly raping the blond woman in some sandy arroyo until she fainted or was dead, and he knew that his cousin was in this all the way.

But Al Hunt had one major shortcoming that could not be ignored. He drank too much and too often. And when he got drunk, he got yappy and he liked to brag. If they came into a lot of money off the dead woman and a Hopi horse race, Whitfield was pretty sure his cousin would go on a bender for weeks, and sooner rather than later he'd be spilling his guts about raping the marshal's wife and how they'd killed both the marshal and the blonde.

That, Whitfield knew, was something that would put a noose around his own neck. So any way he looked at this, only one of them was going back to Flagstaff, and he was going to make sure it was his own suddenly much wealthier self. And while he'd suffer some remorse and even feel some guilt about betraying his cousin Al, remorse was something that faded with time. Getting hanged was something that gave a man no time.

"I'm gonna shoot him in the head," Hunt said, more to himself than to his companion. "Or better yet, the throat. I never shot a man in the throat, but I heard they die choking and flopping around like a chicken with its head lopped off."

"Shoot the marshal in the chest," Whitfield ordered. "Put your first bullet through his heart."

"Not much fun in doin' it that way."

"The hell with fun!" Whitfield snapped. "Just kill him

with the first shot. If he's still alive, you can scalp him or cut off his balls. Slit his throat . . . hell if I care. But put the first bullet through his chest."

"All right," Hunt said, not looking very happy. "But you had better catch the mare."

"I will. Now, let's just shut up and start gettin' our minds right on what we're about to do to that big bastard who killed my brother."

"No offense, Carl, but your brother was meaner than a rattlesnake and—"

"Shut up!"

Al Hunt clamped his jaw tight, and his hand went to the smooth stock of his rifle. *Maybe*, he thought, *I could kill Carl too and take the woman, the buckskin, and all the money for myself. Ride off with her to California or up to the Comstock Lode, take my pleasures wherever they might be found. Sell the blond bitch to a high-class whorehouse when I tire of her.*

Yeah, Al thought, that was something to consider all right.

A short time later, they drew rein north of the gap, and Whitfield said, "All right, you get first shot and you'd better make it count."

"I will. All you have to worry about is catching up that buckskin race horse that you been braggin' about so we can take her on over to the Hopi Reservation and win us a big horse race."

"I'll do it," Whitfield vowed. "Just wait until he's right in the middle of the gap there and can't go nowhere but forward or backward."

"He ain't goin' forward or backward," Hunt snapped. "The only place that big son of a bitch is going is *down*! Straight down into everlasting hell."

Whitfield nodded and set off at a trot that would take him around to the other side of the gap between the sun-baked low hills. Al was the better marksman, but it didn't hurt to be ready with his own rifle in case the man should happen to miss his kill shot.

Chapter 9

Longarm's full attention was directed northward, and his mind was on how to handle what he might encounter up ahead. Billy Vail had told him that the stakes were very high and that Judge Milton Quinn and his young wife were friends of the President of the United States. It all sounded bad to Longarm; even worse after learning that three riverboat men had been murdered. And then there was the matter of Heidi . . . and how to keep her safe from harm.

So as he rode into the gap between the low, barren hills, Longarm wasn't as fully alert to danger as normal. And if it hadn't been for the buckskin mare suddenly twisting her head around and pointing those small, black-tipped ears at something off to his right, Longarm would have been drilled through the heart.

But the mare's slight hesitation of movement and the snort that exploded from her nostrils caused Longarm to glance from side to side just as the man he instantly recognized as Carl Whitfield and another smaller man on his left jumped up with rifles.

"Ya!" Longarm shouted, bending low in the saddle and sending the mare into a hard run in order to escape his death trap. "Ya!"

The mare shot forward like a cannonball, ears flattening against her head, neck stretched out, and legs reaching out to cover ground. The ambushers were caught by surprise, unprepared for the mare's explosive burst of speed. They both fired and missed.

Longarm drew his six-gun and as he passed the two men, he opened fire, emptying his gun at the closer and larger target, Carl Whitfield. The liveryman staggered, dropped his rifle, and collapsed, even as his partner fired a shot that struck Longarm high up in the back and nearly knocked him from his saddle.

"Ya!" Longarm shouted, dropping his gun and desperately grabbing for his saddle horn.

The buckskin mare ran like the wind and Longarm heard one last rifle shot, then he was out of range and hanging on for his life. The mare had veered off the road and was crashing through brush and leaping over rocks. On and on she ran, until at last Longarm was able to exert some pull on her reins and she stopped, heavily lathered and breathing hard.

"Dammit," Longarm weakly whispered, trying to reach around to his back and feel the bullet hole.

He couldn't quite reach that far behind, but the back of his shirt was wet with warm blood and he knew that he was in desperate shape and would bleed to death if he didn't get the wound plugged.

Longarm gazed around him and saw nothing but rock-strewn hills, a few struggling piñon and juniper pines, sage and rabbit brush. While the mare struggled to regain her breath, Longarm sat in his saddle growing weaker by the moment, as his mind whirled an endless circle trying to figure out what he had to do in order to stay alive.

After several minutes, he glanced back over his shoulder to see if the other rifleman had followed his erratic trail into this wild and barren country. Longarm couldn't see anyone, but that didn't mean at least one of the ambushers wasn't on his trail.

Had he somehow managed to kill Carl Whitfield? Longarm knew that if he had fatally shot the liveryman, it had been out of dumb luck. He'd been under heavy fire and on the back of a racing horse when he'd unloaded his pistol toward Whitfield. But maybe he had really gotten lucky and killed the bastard, and that would make it a little easier if he was about to die out here on this vast and desolate Navajo reservation.

His head was nodding lower and he was gripping the saddle horn with both fists, knowing that if he fell off the mare, he was as good as dead. Suddenly, Longarm heard the ominous sound of a rattlesnake close by. He looked down and saw the viper not six feet away, coiled up in the shade of a rock, ready to strike out at the mare's leg. The buckskin jumped into the air and hit the ground running. Longarm managed to hang on, but only for a moment, and then his strength was gone and he let go of his saddle horn and went spiraling down into darkness.

Two miles back at the gap, Al Hunt knelt beside his dying cousin. "You're an unlucky bastard," Hunt said. "That big federal marshal was hit and shootin' blind. No way should you be gut-shot like this. You just had some terrible luck is all."

Carl Whitfield stared up at a blue and cloudless sky,

trying to hold on to life. "I was *never* lucky," he gasped. "And now I'm going to die out here in this hell."

"Yeah," Al Hunt said rather matter-of-factly, "I'm afraid that's the way it's going to happen. You're gut-shot, and there ain't a thing to be done for it except for you to just up and die."

Whitfield grabbed his cousin's wrist and gave it a powerful squeeze. "That marshal couldn't have gotten very far. He was hit bad and bowed up in his saddle. I saw the blood gushin' out of his back."

"I killed him for sure," Hunt said, feeling very proud of himself. "No doubt about that."

Carl Whitfield was a big man and he wasn't dying easy. "Al!"

"Yeah?"

"After I die, take me back to Flagstaff and use my thirty dollars to give me a decent burial." Wild fear captured his battered face. "Swear that you won't leave my body out here where the animals will eat me!"

"I'll take you back," Al solemnly promised. "And I'll see you get buried near your brother, only with a better headstone.

"And . . ." Whitfield was struggling for his last breath and they both knew it. "Al, you gotta do something else for me."

"Name it."

"Write on the headstone that . . ."

Whatever Carl Whitfield wanted on his headstone was lost as his voice and his heavyset body shivered into a deathly stillness.

Al Hunt wasn't a big man, but he was cunning and deadly. He was also practical, and he was already thinking about that rich blond woman that he and his rifle had just made a widow. Why couldn't he still take her? And now there would be no question of who would hump her first.

"Why not?" he asked himself out loud as he stood and surveyed the inhospitable and empty landscape. "But first I'll have to get rid of Carl's body. Git rid of his horse and saddle too. Leave no trace of what happened here and head for the stagecoach stop and just wait for the woman to show up. She's never seen me. I can still have her and her money if I play my cards right."

A smile formed on his ferretlike face, and he snorted with nearly gleeful anticipation. All his life he'd been the follower, the one that sucked hind tit. Carl had been the smart one who had bought the livery and made a decent living. Now, by gawd, he could have someone write a last will and testament giving *him* the Flagstaff stable and anything valuable that went with it.

"Ha!" Al Hunt laughed, seeing how everything was going to fall into his hands. The rich, blond woman, her money, expensive jewelry, and even his cousin Carl's Flagstaff stable.

He'd have it *all*!

Al hurried over to the horses. He was a damn good cowboy and had a rope tied to his saddle. He gathered both of the horses up and led his cousin's bay over to Carl's body.

"You're too damn big for me to lift you up and over your horse, so I'll have to drag you a ways off."

Al tied one end of the rope to the saddle horn and the other around Carl's ankles just above his boots. The boots were pretty nice, so Al took a moment to try them on, but they were much too large for his small feet. So he put his own down-at-the-heel boots back on, remounted his horse, grabbed the reins of Carl's horse, and looked back at his cousin's blood-soaked corpse. "Carl, you sure do look like shit," he said, leading both horses out of the gap in the hills then up through the sagebrush. Twice, Carl's big body got hung up in brush and Al had to dismount and drag it sideways, grunting and cussing. But eventually, he dragged the corpse for almost two miles, until he found a deep and obscure arroyo.

"This ought to do," he said to the battered and gray-faced man. "Ain't quite a nice grave in Flagstaff, but you won't know the difference and I don't rightly care. Why waste the money on a dead man that always tried to boss me around?"

Al untied the rope and tethered both horses to a stunted piñon pine tree. He collected his cousin's six-gun and money then spent an hour covering his body with a heavy mound composed of rocks, sticks, and pieces of deadwood. When he was satisfied that the body would never be found way the hell out on the reservation, he mounted his horse and led Carl's bay a few miles out into the wilderness, where he reluctantly shot the animal.

Al was tough as rawhide, lean as a desert coyote, and quick as a cat. He rolled a smoke and studied the dead horse, wishing he could have taken it over to that Hopi trading post at Keams Canyon and sold the animal, but that would have tied him to the death not only of his cousin, but also of the missing federal marshal.

"This way, I'm free and clear. Just got to find someone to write me up Carl's last will and testament and get me some of that blond woman. Ought not to be too hard, I reckon."

Al Hunt rode back to the gap where they'd waited in ambush. He found a dead limb from a tree and took his time wiping out all evidence of the ambush and the death of his cousin. Satisfied, he backed up to his horse, wiping out his footprints as he went, and mounted his horse.

"Let's go," he said, pushing the animal into an easy gallop. "We got to get to that stagecoach station and have a little fun before the *real* party begins!"

Chapter 10

The Navajo shepherd, his sixteen-year-old son, and two thin black-and-white dogs were moving their small flock across the dry and seemingly desolate reservation. The sheep were long-haired and produced excellent wool in addition to being a source of meat to the People . . . the Dine. It was a warm afternoon, and when they pushed their vocal flock over a rocky ridge, they heard a single rifle shot off in the distance.

Thinking it might have been one of their own people in trouble and in need of help, the father left the son and rode his pony toward the sound of the shot. What he saw next was very troubling. A man on a horse was jamming his rifle into his saddle boot and riding away to the north while a horse on the ground was in the middle of its death throes.

The old man did not understand this, and something told him that there was a great danger if he were seen by the departing horseman. So he rode behind the hill and waited a little while, and then he trotted over to the dead horse, dismounted, and examined the animal. He would, of course, take the good saddle, which was much better than his own, and the bridle, saddlebags, and the rope. But as he examined the dead horse, he could see nothing wrong with its feet or legs, and he could not understand why anyone would kill such a valuable and healthy saddle horse.

The old man needed help to remove the saddle, the off stirrup of which was pinned under the weight of the dead animal, so he rode back to his son, whose name was Henry, and explained the situation.

Henry listened without interruption and then said, "The dogs will protect the flock. I will come with you and we will get the saddle. This is a good day for us, eh, Father?"

"It might be a good day, but it also might be a very bad day. Something is not right."

"Did the rider see you?" Henry asked, concerned about his father.

"No."

Henry was a handsome, confident young man. "Then there is nothing to worry about."

So the father and the son rode their ponies over to the dead horse, and after a great amount of pulling and scraping away dirt, they removed the saddle. Henry looked up and saw buzzards circling. He rode a short loop around the dead horse.

"Something is not right here. I feel an evil spirit close by."

"Then we should hurry away!"

But Henry was a curious young man. "You go," he said. "I will follow the tracks. Maybe we will find another dead horse and a good saddle for me."

The old man, whose name was Shonto, did not like this idea, but he could not deny the fact that Henry's saddle was just a few scraps of rotting leather. So he said, "Be careful, my son."

Henry then galloped off on his small roan pony. He had ridden only a short way when the tracks dipped into a deep arroyo. And it was then that he saw the mound of rocks and brush. A chill passed through his lean and shirtless body. Henry said a quick prayer that he would not be killed or harmed. He knew without any doubt that a dead person was under the mound and that something was very wrong, because white people did not bury their dead in lonely arroyos.

Once more Henry rode around in a circle, and once more he set off to the west, with buzzards coming lower and lower. He came to a gap in the hills. Dismounting, he spent an anxious half hour reading the signs of a fight and seeing dark, clotted blood on the dirt and also where a rider had raced away into the brush.

"I will offer a prayer," Henry said, feeling even greater evil at this place. "And go back to my father and the flock."

But after his fervent prayer, Henry could *not* turn back to his flock. He was a very curious Navajo and he was hoping for a fine saddle like his father had just discovered. So he followed the tracks into the brush for two miles, and that is when he spotted the beautiful buckskin mare standing with her head up and her ears pricked forward in his direction.

"This is not a mustang," Henry said to himself. "This fine horse wears a saddle. But where is its rider?"

Henry had an old black powder pistol stuck in his belt. It was a Navy Colt and he was good with it, although it was prone to misfiring. Drawing his pistol, he rode toward the buckskin, which showed no inclination to gallop away.

And then Henry saw the very big man lying on his back in the rocks and brush. Ants had already begun to crawl across the white man's bloodless face. Henry slowly dismounted and returned his pistol back behind his belt. He looked at the buckskin mare, and his heart jumped with happiness because this was an extremely fine horse and saddle.

And now it was all his!

The man twitched, and a big hand slapped weakly at the ants crawling on his face. Henry jumped back and yanked his pistol out, then cocked it and pointed it at the big white man.

"Who are you!" he cried.

The man's lips moved, and then his hand slipped under his vest, and when it appeared again, there was a shiny United States marshal's badge.

Henry didn't know what to do!

He went over to the man and stared down at his face. The man opened his eyes, barely, and whispered, "Help me."

Henry whirled around and looked to the east. He wished more than anything that Shonto was with him now, because he would have a better idea of what to do next.

"Help . . . me!"

Henry faced a hard decision, and he took a moment to bow his head and pray for the right answer. He did *not* want to help this man. The white man's law was very complicated, and if this man lived, bad things could befall not only himself but his family. Maybe the lawman would even decide that he, Henry, had shot him.

"Please" was the urgent whisper.

Henry had a goatskin bag of water. He grabbed it from what passed as a saddle and opened the stopper. "Drink," he ordered, cradling the man's head in one hand and pouring water into his mouth.

Longarm drank and drank. The water was bitter, but

it was wet, and he slapped some of it on his sunburned face to revive his senses. "I was shot in the back and need your help."

Henry did not want to roll the big man over and look at the bullet wound. "You are probably going to die."

"Maybe not."

Henry wasn't sure what to do next. His hogan was at least six miles away over rough ground . . . his father, about five miles.

"What can I do?"

"A wagon."

"We do not have a wagon. Only sheep."

"A travois. Make a travois."

Henry stood up and walked around in a small, worried circle. He had helped Shoto make a travois once to move his mother to the reservation headquarters, where there was a doctor. He could make one now . . . but *should* he?

Longarm opened his eyes wider and battled his pain. He wondered if the young Navajo was going to help him, or kill him and steal his belongings.

"If you help me," Longarm managed to croak, "I will repay you well."

"With money?"

"Or that buckskin mare."

"I would rather have the mare and your saddle."

"Then it will become yours."

"I will make a travois," Henry said, knowing that he would . . . in the end . . . have had no choice but to help this lawman, or else live the rest of his life riddled with guilt and maybe also cursed.

Henry fired three shots from his old pistol, which he knew would bring his father on the run. Then he set about making the travois using his wool saddle blanket and cutting long poles. He was sure that his father would make changes in the travois and make it better, but he didn't want to sit by the white man, who might die at any minute. If that happened, the man's powerful spirit might consume Henry and drive him into screaming madness.

Chapter 11

Longarm awoke to the sound of a baby crying and a woman's soft, almost cooing voice. The hogan was dim, but a shaft of sunlight was now shining in his eyes through the doorway. The Navajo woman saw him try to sit, so she scooped up her infant and hurried outside. Moments later, the same young man that Longarm remembered offering to give his horse to now appeared with an older Navajo at his side.

"Who are you?" Shonto asked in passable English.

He took a couple of deep breaths to clear his head. "My name is Custis Long. United States Marshal Custis Long. I'm from Denver, Colorado, and I was ambushed."

The Indians exchanged glances, then the younger one said, "I did not shoot you and neither did my father."

"I know that," Longarm told them, feeling very weak. "Two men from Flagstaff ambushed me. I think I killed one, but the other escaped."

"I found the dead one's body," Henry offered. "It was hidden under rocks and brush."

Longarm processed this information for a moment. "Did you see the one that got away?"

Shonto nodded and pointed to the north.

"How bad am I hurt?"

Henry turned around, and he was supple enough of limb that he could reach behind his back and put his finger on a spot up near the shoulder blades.

"Did you already dig the bullet out?"

"Bullet pass through," Shonto said, making a motion away from his own body. "Much blood in sand."

Longarm knew that he had about two days before the stage would pass anywhere close to this part of the reservation. He lay back down on the thin, straw pallet and closed his eyes. "I will give you the buckskin mare and my saddle as promised. You have my word on that."

Henry didn't believe it. "White man lie, mostly."

"Not this one," Longarm said weakly. "But I need to catch the stage going up to the Grand Canyon. It should come through in two days. Can you take me there?"

"You might die on travois. Plenty rough country."

"I'll take my chances on the buckskin mare," Longarm told them closing his eyes.

The two Navajo men said nothing but left the hogan so that they could go off and talk about this among themselves. Longarm felt so tired he fell asleep as the baby began to cry again.

Two days later, Longarm was lifted from his pallet and carried out to his horse then hoisted into his saddle. He clung to the saddle horn and hung his head, fighting off dizziness and nausea. "Let's go," he told the two Indians. "I can't afford to miss that stagecoach."

When the mare began to walk, Longarm struggled not to lose consciousness. He figured that the Indians would take him to the gap where he had been ambushed and through which the stagecoach would have to pass. And, to his way of thinking, that could not be more than five or ten miles.

However, it seemed more like a hundred miles of agony before the man and his son finally called a halt and helped Longarm down from the buckskin mare. They assisted him over to a large boulder where he could sit in shade and await the stagecoach, and they were considerate enough to give him his rifle, canteen, pack, and supplies.

"Will the stagecoach come through soon?"

Henry glanced up at the sun and then down at Longarm. "Not long. If you die, will the white men come after us?"

"No."

"How would they know that we did not kill you if you are dead?" Shonto asked, face furrowed deep with worry.

It was a question that Longarm couldn't answer. "I'm not fixin' to die," he carefully explained. "If I was going to die, I would have done it by now. Take my horse and saddle and go in peace. You have kept your promise, and now I keep mine."

Henry smiled and knelt down in front of Longarm so he could look the white man straight in his eyes. "You have a paper?"

Longarm immediately understood what the Navajo wanted. "As a matter of fact, I do. And a pencil. I'll write you a bill of sale so that if you are ever questioned about the mare and the saddle, it will say that I gave them both to you of my own free will."

"Good!"

Longarm found the pencil and paper and scribbled out the bill of sale and gave it to Henry along with some good advice. "Don't take that mare into Flagstaff or someone will want to take her away from you even if you show them what I just wrote."

Henry nodded with understanding.

"And put the paper I just signed in a safe place where it will not get wet or damaged."

Again, the young Navajo nodded, before he climbed to his feet and hurried to the buckskin. Stroking the mare's neck, he looked to be about the happiest man on earth. So obvious was Henry's joy at owning the mare and saddle that Longarm could not help but feel good for a few moments. He would, of course, have to pay John Wallace a hefty price for the horse and saddle, but the Navajo shepherds had saved his life and he didn't begrudge them a thing.

The pair waved and rode off, leaving Longarm to sit in the shade of the rock and wait. He couldn't imagine how upset Heidi would be when she saw how terrible he looked, but he'd face that hill to climb when the stagecoach arrived. Until then, he just wanted to take a nap.

Chapter 12

The Flagstaff to Grand Canyon stagecoach was loaded to capacity when Heidi was helped on board by John Wallace. "Mrs. Long, I sure do hope that you'll have a comfortable day," the stagecoach owner said before he closed the door. "We're full up and it's gonna be a mite crowded on this run, but just settle in and enjoy the scenery."

Heidi sat down next to an older woman and smiled at her fellow passengers. On her side of the coach facing the rear was a gentle-looking older couple in their sixties who nodded in friendly greeting. Across from her sat a rough and dangerous-looking young man wearing two pistols, and beside him sat what Heidi decided was a mismatched couple. The gentleman was tall, well dressed, and quite the dandy, and he looked to be approaching forty. He had swarthy good looks, a hooked nose, dark piercing eyes, and straight black hair, and he was wearing a fine derby hat and a white starched shirt and collar. He also wore two large gold rings and a diamond stickpin in his tie, and his black boots were polished to a high shine. He was clean-shaven and Heidi sized him up as a successful gambler or perhaps a prosperous saloon owner. The woman sitting right next to him was very young and pretty . . . probably not much older than twenty. She wore too much makeup and kept her eyes downcast as if she were studying something no one else could see in her lap. Heidi thought she detected a dark bruise under one of her eyes but couldn't be sure because it was heavily powdered.

It was the dandy who first introduced himself while removing his derby and placing it on his lap then flicking off a speck of dirt. "My name is Frankie Virden, and this young lady at my side is my . . . fiancée, Miss Carrie Blue."

Heidi smiled at the cowed-looking woman, hoping to lift her spirits. "You're very pretty, my dear."

The girl glanced up for an instant, managing a grateful smile. "Thank you, ma'am."

"My name is Mrs. Heidi Long," she said, trying to get the girl to relax and open up just a little. "Carrie, have you been to the Grand Canyon before?"

The girl nodded unenthusiastically. "Quite a few times."

Frankie Virden jumped back into the conversation. "We're going up to the Grand Canyon on business. I have just opened a saloon a few miles east of Lees Ferry, along with a hotel, to entice and entertain the growing number of tourists. I'm betting that tourism will grow faster than weeds and in a few years I'll be raking in the money."

When Heidi said nothing, Frankie Virden motioned toward the young man who had not yet said a word. "This is Seth and he's my . . . uh, assistant."

Seth looked at Heidi's face, then her bosom, and grinned wolfishly. "Mighty nice to have such attractive company on this run, ma'am."

Heidi gave him no reply. She immediately judged that Seth was the kind of person to be avoided at all costs, and she guessed that he was more of a bodyguard or gunman than any kind of assistant.

"We'll be stopping at the Cameron Trading Post soon, and there we can stretch our legs and take some refreshments. You ladies can also use the powder room while Seth and I take some liquid refreshment."

"You sound," Heidi said, turning back to the wealthy man with the dark, glittering eyes, "as if you are quite familiar with this stagecoach trip."

"Oh, I am! I've been coming up here several times a month with Carrie and Seth. I have to make sure that my interests are being well served. I'm sure that you'll enjoy staying at my Rimrock Hotel."

Heidi had not discussed where they would stay with Longarm, so she said nothing.

"And Mrs. Long," Virden added, "if there is anything I can do to make this trip more comfortable for you or your marshal, please let me know."

Heidi noticed that Frankie Virden's teeth were bonewhite, straight, and perfect. He was certainly attractive, in a rather predatory way, and well mannered, but she sensed that he had a dark side that would not be hard to expose.

"I'm sure that my husband and I will be just fine," Heidi said, managing a smile.

She had turned away from Virden, to the older couple. "And you are?"

"I'm Mr. Elmer Potter and this is my wife, Emily.

We're on our way up to see the Grand Canyon for the very first time. We'll be staying at Mr. Virden's new hotel and viewing the canyon as much as we can. We're only visiting Flagstaff for the summer and plan to return to Boston in the fall." Elmer squeezed his wife's chubby hand. "I have to confess that Emily and I are celebrating our fortieth wedding anniversary in a few days."

"Congratulations!" Virden and Heidi said at the same time.

"Ah, marriage," Frankie Virden said with a warming smile. "When it works, it must be like heaven. But when it doesn't work . . . well, trust me it can be hell."

Heidi looked to the young woman but she didn't so much as blink an eye. Maybe, Heidi thought, she is a prostitute who is currently at the head of the line for Virden's affections. That could explain why she seemed so withdrawn and even afraid. It might also explain that black eye.

"Mrs. Long," Seth said, folding his arms across his chest and tipping back his black Stetson, "I understand that your husband is a United States marshal and that you are from Denver."

"That's true," she said, knowing that there was no point in denying what had obviously become common knowledge.

"How come your husband, the marshal, didn't ride along with us?"

"Seth," Virden warned, "that is really none of our business."

"Well," Seth continued, "it *could* become our business."

"Seth!" There was steel in Virden's voice.

"I just mean," Seth said, "that everyone knows that a

judge and his pretty young wife have gone missing up by the Colorado River. And I don't mean to upset anyone, but there have been—"

"I think you've said enough!" Frankie Virden hissed.

Seth didn't seem in the least bit intimidated. He held up his hands and smiled at everyone. "Folks, I'm just makin' a little friendly conversation by tellin' everyone what they already know and askin' why this lady's husband, who beat the hell out of Carl Whitfield, didn't come along with us. I meant no harm nor disrespect, Frankie."

Frankie Virden wasn't buying it, and his face was tight with anger. "Why don't you just button your lip, Seth?"

"No cause to get upset, Boss."

All the others seemed to glance down at their laps or out the window, and there was a tension in the stagecoach as it rolled and bounced along, heading north.

They stopped at the Cameron Trading Post, and they all exited the coach and made their way inside. When Frankie headed off with Seth, Heidi joined Carrie Blue, and together they went to find some place to relieve themselves and then wash and have something to eat.

"It gets damned dusty up ahead," Carrie said in a small voice. "After we cross over the Little Colorado, the country becomes drier and we'll have to pull the shades down or the dust will swirl up inside the coach. One time we had to do that and it was a really hot day and I damn near died of the heat."

"Where will we stop for the night?"

"Mr. Wallace has someone waiting about fifteen miles up the road, at a stage stop. He's got two small bunkhouses, one for men and one for us women. There's also a kitchen and a few other things, but it's pretty humble. They'll change horses there and feed us tonight and early tomorrow morning before we get back under way."

"This isn't exactly an easy trip, is it?" Heidi said.

"I *hate* this trip," Carrie Blue snapped with surprising anger. "And I don't like going up to the Canyon and the Colorado River, either."

"Why not?"

The girl started to explain, then froze into silence when she saw Virden and Seth approach. "Please just forget I said that," she whispered. "Don't tell Frankie or Seth what I told you."

"I won't. I promise."

An hour later they were back in their places on the stage-coach as it rumbled along, and everyone grew sleepy as the day warmed and the dust began to thicken. Suddenly, however, they heard a shout from up top where John Wallace and his driver were seated.

"Whoa! Whoa!"

"What the hell?" Seth asked, sticking his head out of the window and peering through the dust up ahead. "There's a body up there by the road!"

"Is it a Navajo?" Frankie asked.

"Nope. Mrs. Long, I hate to tell you this, but it's your husband."

Heidi felt her heart drop to her feet. It was all she could do not to cry out with alarm. Instead, she bit her lip, almost hard enough to make it bleed, and gripped her purse. "Is he . . . really dead?" she heard herself ask.

"Nope," Seth told them all after another few minutes. "He's moving, but barely."

"Oh my," Heidi whispered.

Carrie Blue leaned across the coach and took her

hands. "If he's moving, then he's alive and we'll take care of him."

Heidi nodded. "But I'll bet the nearest doctor is way back in Flagstaff."

Carrie didn't deny the fact. Instead, she just squeezed Heidi's hands more firmly and then gently touched her cheek. Heidi bowed her head and tried not to cry.

Chapter 13

Longarm was weak as a kitten when they gathered around him. John Wallace had set the brake on the stage and was now offering him water from a canteen. "Good gawd, Marshal Long, what happened!"

"I was ambushed by two men . . . One of them I'm sure is dead, because he was shot worse than I was."

"Did you recognize them?"

"Yeah. The man I shot and almost certainly killed was Carl Whitfield. I have no idea who the other rifleman was."

Everyone glanced around, and finally Frankie Virden asked the question that was on all their minds. "Where's Carl Whitfield's body if you actually killed him?"

Longarm looked up at the dandy and ignored the question. "Heidi," he said, "I was shot, but the bullet passed in one side of me and out the other. A couple of Navajo men found and took me to their hogan for a few days, where their women used medicine to help staunch the bleeding and stave off a fever or infection. They saved

my life, and in return, I gave the kid my horse and
saddle."

"You *gave* him my best horse?" John Wallace asked,
clearly shocked and displeased.

"It was the right thing to do. He and his father could
have gotten into a lot of trouble by helping me, and I wasn't
forgetting that one of the ambushers got away clean."

"And you've no idea of who he might be?" Virden
asked.

"No."

"Or where Carl Whitfield's body can be found?"

Longarm rolled his head side to side. "The young
Navajo whose name I'm not going to speak, said that he
found a fresh grave . . . or rather a fresh pile of rocks and
brush laid over a body. I'm sure that Whitfield is lying
under that pile. He and his father also said that the other
ambusher shot a good horse, which was probably the one
that Carl Whitfield was riding."

"Why would he shoot a good horse if he could have
taken it to some trading post and gotten money for the
animal?"

"Who are you?" Longarm asked.

"My name is Seth, and I asked you a question."

Longarm judged Seth to be a gunman and someone
that rode both sides of the fence when it came to obeying
the law. "I'll answer your question, Seth, but next time
you'd better show some manners."

"Marshal," the young man growled, "you're hardly in
any shape to tell me or anyone else how to act."

Longarm's handlebar mustache twitched and he stared
up at the younger man. "I'm not going to be under the
weather very long, Seth. That's something you had *better*
keep well in mind."

Frankie Virden scowled and said, "Seth did ask a good

question. Why do you think the other man shot Carl Wakefield's horse?"

"So it wouldn't tie him to the ambush that they laid for me," Longarm replied.

The stagecoach owner said, "There isn't a doctor up at the Grand Canyon, Marshal. I suppose that I'd better turn the stagecoach around and head on back to Flagstaff."

"No!" Longarm lowered his voice. "The Navajo gave me some herbs to stew for a poultice. They said that the wound would heal clean and without infection. Heidi, would you mind?"

"Of course not!"

"You're staying at my new hotel," Virden announced. "There are some girls there that will give you all the help you'll need."

"I'll be glad to help, too," Carrie offered, looking to her supposed fiancé to see if he would have an objection. "I'll help do whatever I can."

Virden shot her a disapproving glance. "You have other things to do, Carrie. I need you close at hand, and I'm sure that the marshal will have all the help he needs without your interference."

Carrie's face fell as she hurried away. Heidi looked up at the gambler and hotel owner and she was seething inside. "I don't know what your game is, Mr. Virden, but I can tell you right now that I don't like the way you're treating that girl and I don't like you . . . either."

Virden laughed. "Well, Mrs. Long, try to imagine how little your opinion on *anything* matters to me."

"All right," John Wallace interceded, "I think we've heard just about enough of this squabbling. Let's help the marshal into the stagecoach." He looked into Longarm's gray eyes. "Are you sure that you don't want me to turn around and head straight back to Flagstaff?"

"Positive," Longarm firmly replied. "And I'll make sure that you are repaid for the value of that buckskin mare and saddle."

"I'd appreciate that," Wallace said. "She was pretty special to me, and I was afraid that something bad might happen to her. Turns out it happened to you instead."

"For what it's worth," Longarm told the stagecoach owner and liveryman, "the young Navajo that now owns her will take very good care of the mare. He was not much more than a kid, and when I gave him the horse and wrote him out a legal bill of sale, I thought he was going to jump over the moon with happiness."

"Glad to hear it," Wallace said, still not looking a bit happy. "Most of these Navajo Indian ponies are treated pretty poorly, and a lot of them are underfed."

"That won't happen to the buckskin," Longarm assured the man.

"Okay," Wallace said. "Let's get you up into the coach and then on up to the Grand Canyon and that new hotel." He looked around at the group. "One of you gentlemen is going to have to sit up top on the driver's seat with me."

When none of the men volunteered, Carrie Blue said, "I'd enjoy a better view and more fresh air. I'll gladly join you up there."

The stagecoach owner scowled at Virden, Seth, and Elmer Potter, but when they refused to meet his eyes he said, "All right, Miss Blue. I'll give you a hand up, and you can sit beside me until we reach the stage stop where we'll change teams and rest up for the night. Until then I'll try to avoid the worst of the potholes and rocks so that you don't get bounced around up there any more than necessary."

"Thank you."

Heidi shot all three of the male passengers a look of pure disgust. "I see that around here they use the term 'gentlemen' very loosely."

Virden and Seth both barked a disdainful laugh. Elmer Potter took his wife's hand and walked away.

They helped Longarm to his feet and assisted him over to the stagecoach. With a little boost from the others, he managed to drag himself up onto a seat and then the others climbed into the coach.

"Here," Wallace said, handing Longarm a good wool blanket. "You can use this to steady and prop yourself up against those cushions. I'm afraid the road north is pretty rough."

"Can't be any rougher than riding over rocks and brush in a travois," Longarm replied. "Let's get moving."

A short while later the coach was rolling along at a steady and ground-eating pace. John Wallace had four good horses in harness, and although the wagon track they followed was narrow and uneven, the animals were in excellent condition and Wallace was an outstanding driver.

"So," he said to Carrie after a time, during which he had considered the ambush and what was going to happen to the marshal, "you and Mr. Virden are engaged to be married?"

Carrie Blue glanced sideways at him and seemed to reach a decision. "Mr. Wallace, just between you, me and those horses? No, we're never going to get married."

"But . . ."

"The truth is, Mr. Wallace, I'm Frankie's woman for the time being and nothing more."

Wallace blushed. "Listen, Miss Blue, I didn't mean to pry or anything. What's going on between you, Mr. Virden, and that character named Seth is simply none of my business."

"It *should* be your business."

Wallace swung his head around to stare at her. "And why is that?"

"Well, what if Frankie were to tell you one of these days that he was tacking on a charge for every passenger you bring up to his hotel?"

"What kind of a *charge*?"

"Ten dollars a person."

John Wallace made a face. "And why on earth would I pay the man ten dollars per passenger?"

"Because," Carrie said, "if you don't, then Frankie will buy a stagecoach and bring his own passengers up to the hotel and he won't let any of your passengers stay there for even one night."

Wallace felt his gut tighten and he saw that such a rotten thing could be done to him. "But . . . why on earth would he do that?"

"He would do *anything* to make money." She took a deep breath of the clear and heavily scented sagebrush air. "Mr. Wallace, if you tell Frankie what I've just told you, I'm going to be in a lot of trouble."

It was all that the driver could do to ask, "What kind of trouble?"

"*Bad* trouble."

"Meaning another black eye?"

She wrung her hands together. "And much worse."

John Wallace snorted in anger. "Why do you even stay with him and that two-bit gunman named Seth? Why don't you just leave them?"

"And do what?" she asked bitterly. "Become a street prostitute? Maybe work for some madam at a nice whorehouse because I've still got my looks?"

Wallace gulped with embarrassment. "Miss Blue, I didn't mean . . ."

She was angry. "You're a man and you own a stagecoach line and a stable, so you don't understand that women don't have the same chances. Prostitution is my only other future, and . . . and I've decided that it's better to be one man's whore than a whore for hundreds."

"Jaysus," Wallace whispered, snapping the lines and wishing the stagecoach would move faster. "I just didn't . . ."

"Mr. Wallace, you don't go to whorehouses." It wasn't a question but a professional's observation.

"No."

She was looking right through the side of his face. "And you don't have a wife?"

"Had one. She died of diphtheria about three years ago. We were only married eighteen months and we didn't even have time to start a family."

"I'm sorry," Carrie Blue said, expression finally softening. "I never had a husband . . . just men who came and went. Frankie and I have only been together six months, and there are women in Flagstaff who say that's some kind of a long-term record with him."

"That may be true, but it's no life for you."

"It *is* a life," she said fiercely. "And I haven't given up on everything quite yet. Maybe I can walk away from Frankie before he dumps me for a new girl, and maybe I can take some money with me when I go."

They rode along, with the day growing short and a faint pinkness settling into the western sky. Songbirds were flitting in the brush, and they saw a huge bird floating up high against the clouds.

"That sure is a *huge* buzzard," Carrie said, breaking a long silence.

"That's a condor," Wallace told her, relieved to get off the subject of their personal lives. "They have such a huge wingspan that they can glide for hundreds of miles and never flap a wing."

Carrie Blue wiped a tear from her eye. "Got a little dust in it, I think."

"No, you didn't," Wallace said, looking closely at the woman. "We're not in a dusty stretch."

"Well . . ."

"Well, what?"

Carrie thought a moment and then confessed, "I was just wishing I could soar like that over the face of this hard, damned country. Wishin' I could sail on and on and never stop."

"You're envyin' a buzzard?" he asked in an awkward attempt at humor.

"That's *not* a buzzard . . . You just told me it was a condor."

Wallace chuckled. "Big buzzard is what it really is."

"Maybe so," Carrie said as the rest stop for the night, with its adobe cabin, outbuildings, and corrals, finally came into view, "but it can do the thing that I'd most like to do now . . . just fly and fly and never stop until I was on the other side of the whole world."

John Wallace wondered just how much pain Miss Carrie Blue had suffered already. Probably more than he could even imagine or want to imagine.

And then he got to thinking about Frankie Virden and how the son of a bitch was fixin' to put him out of business or charge him a per-passenger rate of ten dollars.

Ten dollars! Why, the fare he charged each way wasn't a hell of a lot more than that.

John Wallace shook his head with worry. He reckoned that maybe Miss Carrie Blue and he were *both* caught in Frankie Virden's clutches.

Chapter 14

Al Hunt watched the stagecoach through a pair of binoculars as it rolled into the little adobe stage stop to rest its passengers for the night. He watched the driver and stage line owner, John Wallace, help a pretty woman down, and for a moment he was sure it was the federal marshal's wife, but then he realized that there was another woman stepping out of the coach along with the other passengers.

So, Hunt thought, there were *two* young women on the stage, but the one that had been in the coach was the rich woman married to the United States marshal. She was the lady that he wanted to capture for his pleasure and for ransom.

"Son of a bitch!" Hunt hissed a moment later as he stared in disbelief at the big marshal being helped out of the stagecoach. "Shit!"

And not only was the federal marshal still alive, he was able to walk with some assistance from his wife.

Al Hunt was lying spread-eagled in the dirt on a hillside, and now he laid his head down on his forearms and

beat the earth in anger and frustration with a bare fist.
How in the world could the marshal still be alive! He'd
shot the man and saw him bend forward as the buckskin
mare raced away into the brush.

Son of a bitch! The marshal was alive . . . no getting
around the fact. But, and this was the good part, it was
clear to see that he was in rough shape.

Hunt lay still while thinking hard. What was he going
to do now? He could ride away and just go back to Flagstaff with his horse and claim he had been given the livery by his late friend and cousin. But if he did that . . .
wouldn't it then be obvious that he must have been with
Carl when the marshal was ambushed?

Of course it would! When the big United States marshal returned to Flagstaff, he would immediately understand that he, Al Hunt, had been the other ambusher at
the gap.

Hunt's mind went through all his alternatives, and he
knew that he was in a desperate fix. After giving the matter some hard thought, he decided that the only thing he
could do to save his ass and to grab possession of his late
cousin's profitable livery stable was to kill the marshal.
Kill him somewhere out in this rough country, and this
time make damn good and sure that the man never
returned to Flagstaff.

As the sun went down and night fell upon the high
desert country, Hunt climbed to his feet, slapped the dirt
off himself, and decided that he had one big advantage,
and that was that the federal marshal had not seen his
face and had no idea that he had been one of the two men
involved in the ambush.

"I'll just circle around that stage stop and go on up to
the Colorado River and Grand Canyon," he decided out
loud. "And when that stagecoach pulls in to Frankie

Virden's Rimrock Hotel, I'll act like I'm just another tourist. And then I'll pick my time and kill that marshal and have his rich widow all for myself just as poor old Carl and I had planned . . . Only Carl won't be around to have his pleasures."

That decided, Al Hunt climbed back on his horse and gave wide berth to the stage stop as he purposefully rode on to the north. He would make a dry camp tonight, and tomorrow, when the stagecoach rolled up to unload its passengers, there he'd be looking just like everyone else when those two pretty women arrived. He'd made the mistake of not getting on his horse and going after the badly wounded marshal to finish him off somewhere in the sagebrush.

He'd not make that same mistake a second time, by gawd!

Longarm was damned glad to get out of the coach and onto a cot at the stage stop. He was weak and light-headed, but he knew that he simply needed a bit of time to rebuild his strength and replenish a lot of spilled blood.

"So," Heidi asked when they were settled into a little screened-off room and had some privacy to themselves. "What *exactly* happened?"

"I told you . . . I was riding through this gap and I was ambushed. Lucky to get away, and even luckier when a Navajo lad and his father happened to be close enough to get me to their family's hogan. The Navajo women have some very powerful medicine and they pulled me through."

"You're weak as could be," Heidi told him. "Stay here and I'll go to the kitchen and bring you back a plate of hot food."

"Thanks, but I'm not very hungry."

"You *have* to eat in order to regain your strength."
Heidi leaned over and kissed his lips. "Frankie Virden
is no good . . . I saw that the minute he climbed into the
coach with that poor girl he's dragging along to make
himself look good. But Virden does have a new hotel
where we're going, and I'm sure we will be given a private room where you can rest and regain your strength."

"I just need a couple of days," Longarm told her. "Just
a few days to get back to my old self."

"You'll be needing more than a few days," Heidi told
him. "And that's fine."

"No, it isn't fine," he argued, looking up at her. "I'm
a federal marshal, and someone tried, and damn near
succeeded, in killing me. And on top of that, I've got
murders to solve and people to try to find at the Grand
Canyon."

"I understand," Heidi said calmly, "but if you die,
you're not going to do anything, and you'll be leaving me
in one hell of a bad fix."

"Is that what you're *really* worried about?"

"You know that it isn't," Heidi told him. "You know
that I'm better than that."

"I do," he said. "Sorry."

"I'll be back soon with a big plate of something good
for you to eat," she promised as she left his side. "Custis,
just try to close your eyes and get some rest."

"Eat some good food yourself before you come back,"
he told her. "Because, from the way this is starting off,
we're *both* going to need to be in good form."

Heidi stopped and turned. "Why do you say that? I'm
not in any danger."

"Maybe you are," Longarm told her. "You're rich and
beautiful, and those are very rare commodities in this

country. Heidi, you're going to have to be very careful and watch everyone closely. There's only a few reasons anyone would ambush me like they did, and you could be one of those reasons."

"I'll watch out for us both."

"I'm sure that you will," Longarm told her. "This stagecoach is only going to stay at the Grand Canyon overnight and then it will head back to Flagstaff. Maybe you should plan to be on it when that happens."

"Not a chance. Don't even talk about me leaving you after what's happened."

"You're sure?"

"Dead sure," she said, crossing her arms and looking down at him with steel in her eyes.

"All right then. Just remember I tried to talk you into doing the safe thing."

"I've done the 'safe thing' before and it's boring as hell."

That brought a chuckle. "I know what you mean, Heidi. Now go get us some food before it's all gone."

She smiled and left their private little space, and the moment she was out of sight, Longarm pushed himself erect and stood tall. He took several deep breaths and then walked back and forth a few steps, taking measure of his physical condition. To his dismay, he realized that he was pretty unsteady. Hopefully, that would pass in a few days at Frankie Virden's new hotel. It had better pass quickly, because there were lives at stake and deadly men afoot. And there was an ambusher out there someplace who for some reason wanted him dead. Maybe still thought he *was* dead.

Longarm sat down feeling a bit dizzy. He needed to get stronger all right, and he needed to do it quick.

Chapter 15

When the stagecoach arrived at the Rimrock Hotel, on the southern rim of the Grand Canyon, Elmer and Emily Potter were beside themselves with wonder because of the inspiring and majestic view.

"My gawd!" Elmer Potter exclaimed. "Emily, would you just look at that!"

His wife, mouth hanging open, simply stared in amazement. Finally, she said, "It's really, really big, isn't it, Elmer."

"Bigger than any old hole I ever saw!"

"And so many colors . . . Elmer, I just can't get over the *colors*. And look at that little river way down there just like a ribbon of silver. I thought the Colorado was a big river, but it's just a creek is all that it is."

John Wallace left his stagecoach with Carrie Blue so he could join the excited couple. "The Colorado River is low right now, but even so it's a lot bigger than it appears from up here on the rim. When you get down there, it will seem large and powerful. In the springtime it roars so loud that it fills the canyon with a sound louder than a thousand locomotives going through a train tunnel."

Carrie Blue laughed. "Why, Mr. Wallace, you've a poetic streak within you near as wide as that canyon!"

"Ah," he scoffed, "it's just that every time I see the Grand Canyon it takes my breath away and leaves me feeling like I'm small, insignificant, and blessed to behold such a great wonder."

"My," Carrie said, having a little fun with the man, "and I thought you were just a fellow who liked horses and mules."

He laughed and tore his eyes away from the canyon to gaze down at her. "You're a mighty pretty sight yourself, Miss Blue. And don't you ever let anyone forget it."

"I'll try not to."

"Carrie!" Frankie Virden shouted from the porch of his newly constructed hotel. "Dammit, we need some help over here!"

Carrie's smile died, and she hurried over to the Rimrock Hotel, where several people were standing on the porch. She'd been here quite a few times with Frankie and Seth, and she knew that she was expected to be sort of a hostess to the incoming guests. And if there were any of them that were wealthy, she should subtly make sure they understood that she was discreetly available day . . . or night.

Longarm and Heidi stood together looking down at the canyon for several minutes in silence, and then Heidi said, "No matter what happens, seeing this makes it all worthwhile."

"It does," Longarm agreed. "I've been here only twice before, and I still can't quite wrap my mind around the size of the Grand Canyon. And you'll soon realize that the lighting and colors are always changing. One of the times I was here, there was snow dusting the pinnacles, buttes, and steps. Notice how the canyon walls are like stairways instead of just straight up and down in most places?"

"I see that. And where is this Lees Crossing that we have to find?"

"It's a few miles east of us," Longarm told her. "We'll be going there in a couple of days."

"That river looks narrow and shallow enough to ride a horse across it."

"It's a fooler from way up here," Longarm told her. "Believe me when I say we'll need to be ferried across and that the water will be swift and treacherous."

"And you still think we might have to go down it on a raft?" Heidi asked, looking worried.

"I don't know," he said honestly. "In 1869, when the Powell expedition did it for the first time, they almost were lost. Three of the members of that expedition *were* lost."

"Drowned?"

"No," Longarm said. "At Separation Rapids they abandoned the group and climbed up the north rim, never to be seen again."

"Why did they leave?"

"The expedition didn't realize how close they were to coming out of the canyon. They'd been fighting rapids and the river for weeks and were starving. Their rafts had overturned and they'd lost most of their food and they hadn't had any luck hunting or fishing. Even worse, they never knew if around the next bend in that river there would be a big and disastrous waterfall."

"Animals exist down there, don't they?"

"A few mountain goats and sheep and maybe some lizards and rattlesnakes. Not much, though. It is not a very hospitable place down at the bottom of that canyon."

Longarm had to force his eyes from the sight. "Heidi, what do think the temperature might be where we're standing?"

"In the low eighties I should think."

"I agree. And down at the bottom of the Grand Canyon it will be a hundred degrees or more."

She looked up at his face. "Really?"

"Yes. It's a lot hotter down there." Longarm forced what he knew was a poor joke. "Reason being it's closer to hell."

She laughed and almost jabbed him in the ribs before catching herself. "Custis, it's clear that you've lost a lot of blood, but at least you haven't lost your sense of humor."

"No, I haven't," he told her. "Now, I think we should check out Frankie Virden's hotel."

"The Grand Canyon is far more impressive."

"Even so," Longarm said, "we need to get a room, and I'm sure you wouldn't turn down a hot bath, and neither would I."

"I want to change your bandage and use those herbs to make and apply a poultice," she told him. "We have to get you well as soon as possible."

"Amen to that."

The Rimrock Hotel was situated about fifty feet back from the rim of the Grand Canyon, and although it was only a single story tall, it was large and well designed, with a small dining room and lobby facing north so that guests could relax and enjoy the ever changing view of the great chasm. The furniture was rustic, made of pine, and boasted a large and impressive fireplace constructed of the red and yellow sandstone that was so prominent in the canyon.

"Not too bad," Longarm muttered as Frankie Virden, with Carrie Blue on his arm, regaled the new arrivals with the facts about his Rimrock Hotel.

"I've tried to bring a part of the canyon into the hotel for my guests," he was saying. "Note the décor and the furnishings, all of which were designed and constructed to put my guests in the spirit of this wonderful canyon. We are, of course, a work in progress. To date, we've twelve guest rooms, and it's my intention to build a saloon and gaming hall where friendly games of poker, monte, and other gambling can take place for the gentlemen who have that interest and the means to pursue it with great pleasure."

Most of the guests gathered around smiled, but some looked away quickly, leading Longarm to think that they had already been fleeced by Frankie or one of his professional gamblers.

"You will find that we have tried very hard to add variety to the meals we serve, but again, this is not the Waldorf Astoria and as you can well imagine it isn't easy to keep fresh food on hand this far from Flagstaff or other sources of supply."

"Does that mean you'll be feeding us jackrabbit and calling it pheasant?" Elmer Potter asked, making his own attempt at humor.

Frankie Virden's dark eyes flashed with anger. "No, Mr. Potter, it does not. I do have staff that regularly hunt for deer and other wild game that can be brought into my hotel kitchen and prepared with some degree of elegance and taste . . . which I'm sure you would not begin to appreciate."

Elmer Potter and his wife were not brilliant, but they

weren't dumb, and they flushed with anger at the insult.
"We'd like to see our rooms," Elmer managed to say.

"In time," Frankie Virden replied coolly. "In time."

Longarm and Heidi were the first to register, because
it was obvious that he was weak and needed his rest.
When they were shown to their room by Carrie Blue, she
said, "Dinner is always at eight. I'm told that tonight we'll
be having fresh trout. Liquor of all kinds is available, but
it's expensive."

"Champagne and French chardonnay would be very
nice," Heidi said hopefully. "And a bath. A good, hot
bath."

"And whiskey," Longarm quickly added.

Carrie pointed to a big copper bathtub. "I'll have
someone fill the bath as soon as possible, and I'll bring
your bottles as soon as I can," she promised, as she
straightened a bedcover. "I hope you enjoy your stay at
the Rimrock Hotel. I think this particular room is one of
our nicest, and it does have that special window view
toward the canyon, which only half the rooms have for
our guests."

"It's very nice," Heidi said, "and even quite clean. But
what, if I may ask, is *your* role here? Are you doubling
up as your fiancé's maid or . . ."

"Or whatever the traffic will bear and the guests
require," she interrupted, hurrying away.

When they were alone, Heidi tested the mattress and
then joined Longarm in stretching out to relax.
"Custis?"

"Yeah?"

"What is going on with that poor young woman?"

"What do you mean?"

"I mean that she has a black eye that she's tried hard
to cover with powder and that she just told us . . . if I

understood between the lines . . . that she is available to men at a high price."

"Yeah," he said. "I don't think she meant to say that to us just now, but that's what I heard."

"She's very unhappy, and I think she is scared stiff of Frankie Virden and that other man, Seth."

"I suppose you're right."

"I know that I'm right," Heidi said, sitting up and staring at the door. "And when I get the chance, I'm going to try to befriend her and see if there is something I can do to help the poor young woman."

"Even if she has a shady past and is 'available' to the male guests of this hotel?"

"*Especially* if she is in that kind of position," Heidi said with determination. "If she was happy with her choice and this situation, then I'd not interfere, but I think she is very unhappy and in desperate need of help and support."

"If you go to her and Frankie Virden finds out . . . there will be consequences," Longarm warned.

"That *you*, Marshal Long, will most certainly be capable of handling."

"Right again," Longarm told her, realizing that they had independently reached the same conclusions about Virden, Seth, and Carrie Blue. And they both knew that there was a very unsettling and dangerous undercurrent here at the beautiful south rim of the Grand Canyon.

Chapter 16

Al Hunt was already sick and tired of sleeping on the ground, sweating in the bright northern Arizona sun and then at night freezing as the temperatures dropped. He hadn't brought a bedroll and he had almost nothing to eat or drink and it was miserable being camped out on this high plateau. He was hot and dirty, and he stunk so bad that even his horse seemed not to want to be near him, and the animal was slowly starving.

"I *have* to get a room, a bath, a bottle, and a decent meal at the Rimrock Hotel," he muttered as he tightened his cinch and prepared to ride down a hill toward Frankie Virden's hotel.

Hunt had some money, and he knew that Frankie Virden, along with that woman, Carrie Blue, would recognize him the minute he showed up at the hotel, and they'd probably wonder what the hell he was doing way out here. They'd immediately be suspicious and maybe even ask him about the comings and goings of his newly departed cousin Carl, but at this point, tired, hot, and hungry, Al Hunt figured he could come up with the right answers. He knew that Frankie was a ruthless and clever bastard, but Hunt figured he could hold his own and manage to avoid suspicion.

So with his stomach growling and his horse fractious for lack of anything to eat, Al Hunt rode over to the south rim and the Rimrock Hotel, just as the stagecoach was being hitched up for the return trip to Flagstaff.

John Wallace stood beside Carrie Blue, and when they spotted Al coming down to the hotel, they stopped talking and just watched his approach.

"Morning, John, Carrie," Al said in greeting as he dismounted. "Any food or liquor left inside for me?"

Wallace made no pretense of being friendly. He'd never liked this man and saw no point in offering his hand in greeting. "What are you doin' up this way?"

"I'm sort of lookin' for work in these parts," Hunt replied. "Thought maybe Mr. Virden could use another hand."

"He can't," Carrie said shortly. "There is no work for you here."

Al managed not to lose his temper. "Well, Miss Blue, I'd say that is something that Mr. Virden needs to say instead of you. I'll be speaking to him directly, but for now, I think I'll just go inside and see about a room, a bath, and some liquor and food."

Carrie clamped her mouth shut, and when the dirty, smelly man tipped his hat and then entered the hotel, she turned to John Wallace. "He's got a bad reputation and I wish he hadn't shown up."

"I'm sure that Frankie will send him packing unless Al has enough money to pay for a room and his food and liquor."

Carrie nodded. "Frankie would put the Devil himself up if he had gold or greenbacks."

"Yeah, I'm sure that he would," Wallace agreed. He had finished hitching up his team and was already late in heading back, but he was procrastinating. "You know, you could come back on this stage with me," he finally managed to say.

She looked closely at him. "And what would I do to pay for *my* room and board in Flagstaff?"

Wallace toed the ground, feeling uncomfortable. "I don't know," he managed to say. "But I do have a lot of friends in Flagstaff and some of them own businesses. Might be I could help you find honest work."

"'Might be'?" she asked. "But what if you couldn't? What then?"

Wallace scowled. "Dammit, I just can't say for certain."

"Well," Carrie said, "until you can say for certain that I won't be standing on the street with a tin cup in my hand, then I'll have to stay with Frankie."

"I guess," Wallace told her as he turned to leave. "But I sure don't like that very much."

Carrie's expression softened. She looked over her shoulder at the hotel to make certain that no one was watching, then lifted up on her toes and gave John Wallace a quick kiss on the cheek.

He jumped back, eyes wide open with surprise. "Why did you do that?"

"You know why. John, please do look for some honest work for me when you get back to Flagstaff. And if you should find some, despite my . . . my reputation . . . then I'll come back with you on your next run."

"What about Frankie?"

"I'll tell him that I'm leaving him," she said, chin raised. "But I'd want you to be standing at my side when I do it. Otherwise . . ."

"Otherwise the son of a bitch would punch the other eye, eh?"

"Yes," Carrie said, "he would. And worse."

Wallace nodded with understanding. "I'll be back in about a week, and when I am, I'll have found some honest work for you and a place for you to live."

"I hope so," she said. "Good-bye."

John Wallace was a big man, and he knew that he was not handsome. But there was something inside of him saying that he didn't want to say good-bye to Carrie again and that . . . even if he had to sell his business and pack up everything he owned to get away from the gossip . . . he would do it for Miss Blue and then he'd make her an honest woman.

And so, with a look of grim determination, John Wallace climbed up onto his stagecoach and turned it south toward Flagstaff. In one week his life was going to change forever, and he just knew in his heart that it would for the better. Better for him and better for Miss Blue. Neither of them was too old to have a family, and that was really all he had ever wanted in this world.

Al Hunter got a room, a bottle, and a bath, paying up most of his cash. He told the man at the registration desk that he wanted some food delivered to his room along with the drink and hot water.

"I will tell our cook," he said. "Would you also like those clothes to be washed?"

"Hell, yes."

"And what about your horse?"

"How much to feed the mangy son of a bitch for a couple of nights? And I mean feed him and grain him good."

"Fifty cents a night."

Al Hunt gave the man another dollar. "See that he's taken good care of . . . rubbed down and watered before he's fed."

The man nodded and held out his hand. Al swore under his breath and gave him the extra dollar he knew was required if his wishes were to be granted.

An hour later, with a bottle of whiskey in one hand and a bar of soap in the other, Al was enjoying his bath very much when there was a knock at his door. "Who the hell is it!"

"Frankie."

"Come on in, Mr. Hotel Owner!"

Frankie Virden didn't say hello, and he entered with Seth right behind. Frankie shut the door behind him while Seth leaned up against it with his arms folded across his chest. The hotel owner and gambler grabbed the only chair in the room and pulled it up beside the man in the bathtub. "Enjoying yourself, Al?"

Al Hunt splashed a little water across his whiskery, sunburned face. "Sure am!"

"Like my whiskey?"

"It's a helluva lot better than the firewater I'm used to."

"I'll bet it is," Virden said.

"Want a swig?" Al offered his bottle to the man. "I paid for it, but you can have a pull. You too, Seth."

"No, thanks." Virden was not a man to beat around the bush, and so he came right to the point. "Carrie said that you wanted work."

"I damn sure do." Al had decided that this was the only excuse he could use while he waited for the opportunity to finish off the wounded federal marshal and grab the rich woman for a ransom and rutting.

"I never knew you to be much of a worker," Frankie

drawled, glancing back at Seth. "Fact is, your cousin Carl claimed that you were the laziest man in his entire family . . . and also the most treacherous and cunning."

"He did?"

"That's right. Carl didn't have much of anything good to say about you."

"Huh." Al Hunt took a swallow. "Well, Carl was the only one of us that ever amounted to anything, so I guess he's got the right to say what he wants about me."

"He also said you were a purely dangerous little bastard."

Hunt blinked and tried to look offended. "Well I find that hard to believe, Mr. Virden. Was Carl drunk as a loon at the time he said those bad things about me?"

"He was cold sober."

"Huh!"

The whiskey was already working in Al's shrunken, starved belly, hitting him harder and faster than ever before, but this conversation was making him even more thirsty. He didn't like the way it was going and tried to change the subject. "Sure a nice hotel you got here, Mr. Virden."

"Yes it is, and I never thought I'd have the likes of you as a guest."

"Aw, that's a pretty awful thing to say!"

"You're a pretty awful little man." Virden took a cigar from his coat pocket and struck a match to it. "So why *are* you staying here?"

"What do you mean? I told you I was here looking for honest work."

"No," Virden countered. "You told *Carrie* that."

"Same thing, I reckon."

Frankie Virden blew a ring of smoke in Al Hunt's pinched and burned face and smiled. "A man like you doesn't spend money unless he's sure he's going to be getting more of it right back."

Hunt frowned, feeling his heart start to beat a little faster. "Truth of the matter is that I won some money in a card game."

"In Flagstaff?"

"No . . . uh, at the Cameron Trading Post. There were some fellas passin' through and they invited me into a card game and I won all their money."

But Virden shook his head. "I've seen you play cards, Al. You're a lousy player. Reckless as hell."

"Sometimes a man's luck can overcome his inadequacy," Al replied, pleased at his explanation.

He started to take another swallow, but then Frankie glanced around behind him at Seth and gave a short nod. And before Al even realized it, the gunman was striding across the room, slamming his hand down on Al's head, and pushing it underwater.

Al struggled and fought, but the tub was slick and Seth was strong. Al gasped and choked and swallowed bathwater. Finally, Seth released the downward pressure and Al came up gagging.

"What'd you have him do that for, Mr. Virden!"

"I want the truth out of you," the gambler and hotelman said. "And I want it right now."

"But I told you the truth! I won my money at the Cameron Trading Post and . . ."

Frankie nodded to his man, and Seth jumped forward and pushed Al's head back underwater. This time, he held Al under even longer, and when Al's lungs were ready to explode, Seth finally let go.

"Holy shit!" Al cried, coughing and gagging. "What the hell is wrong here! I paid honest money for this room and everything! I don't deserve this kinda shit!"

"The truth," Frankie Virden said, smiling coldly.

Al's bloodshot eyes darted back and forth between the two men. His gun was out of reach and he was helpless. He also knew that Frankie Virden would have his man drown him if he didn't come up with something good and fast.

"All right!" he gasped. "I . . . I didn't win the money at cards."

"Where *did* you get your money and why are you infecting my hotel with your filth?" Virden asked quietly.

Al Hunt swallowed hard and decided that only the truth would save him from being drowned in his own bath like a rat. "Me and Carl ambushed that federal marshal."

Virden's eyebrows arched in a question. "To rob him?"

"No. As you know, Mr. Virden, that marshal beat the living hell out of Carl, and he wanted to get even."

"So you shot and only wounded him, but Carl was killed?"

"Yes, sir. That's just the way it happened. We shot the federal marshal right where you found him when you rode in with the stagecoach. The marshal's horse bolted and he ran off, but I saw the blood fly outa his coat and knew he was a goner."

"Oh, but he *wasn't*. The federal marshal is very much alive."

"I know that now."

"What did you do with your cousin's body?"

"Well, after the marshal killed him, I took old Carl's body out in the desert and found me a deep gully. I buried poor Carl and shot his horse."

"So there wouldn't be any connection between you and your cousin and the ambush."

"Yes, sir."

Al wasn't about to tell this man about his plan to acquire Carl's livery with a fake deed, or about his plan to kill the marshal for good this time and take his wife hostage. "I . . . I know you don't like lawmen either, Mr. Virden. I didn't think you'd mind if we killed him."

"Oh, I don't mind that at all," Virden said. "Only you and that jackass cousin of yours *failed*."

"Could I have that bottle back, sir?"

"Certainly. After all, you paid for it."

"Yes, sir."

"With the money you took off your dead cousin's body before you covered him up out in some ravine."

"Carl would have done the same to me. And what would be the point of leavin' money on a dead man who couldn't spend it?"

"I see your logic, Al. But now we have a big problem."

"I can take care of my problems," Al blurted. "I won't bring you any grief, and I won't hold it against your man there for nearly drownin' me. Honest I won't."

"Is that right?"

"Yes, sir!"

Virden blew another smoke ring in Al's face, and then he stood up and walked around the room a few times, head bowed in thought. Al's heart was really hammering now, and when he looked into Seth's eyes, he saw nothing. No pity, no understanding, no nothing—the same as when you looked into a varmint's cold eyes.

The bath was warm, but Al suddenly shivered.

"Sir, I will do whatever you ask me for very little pay."

"Oh, I know that," Virden said. "Did you come here to kill the marshal out of revenge for the way he beat your cousin?"

"No, sir."

"I'm very glad you said that, because I know that was an honest statement."

"But I *would* kill the marshal, if you asked."

"But you've already failed once."

"It was Carl that messed things up back at that gap between the hills! Not me."

Virden stopped his pacing. "I would like the marshal . . . finished off. It would take care of a big problem for me. Much better if you did it instead of Seth, but either way, I . . ."

"I'll do it! I'll even do it tonight if you want."

"And exactly how would you kill the marshal?"

"I'd creep into his room and stab the big bastard to death in the dark."

"And what about his wife?"

"I'd do her too, if you wanted."

"No," Virden said, "I definitely wouldn't want the woman killed."

"Then I'd cover my face with a mask, kill the marshal, hit the woman in the head but not hard enough to put her under, and I'd run out. In the morning, I'd sit at your breakfast table, and no one would know I'd been the one that stabbed the marshal to death. No one at all."

Frankie Virden looked to Seth. "It's a plan. Simple, but it would probably work. What do you think, Seth?"

"Why not?"

Virden turned back to Al Hunt. "All right. I'll give you a second chance to kill the marshal. But if you fail . . ."

The words left unsaid were enough to suddenly sober Al up as right as rain.

"Give me that bottle," Virden ordered.

"I ain't had enough yet."

"Yes, you have. Do the job right this night and I'll see

that you have enough whiskey money to last you until New Year's Eve."

Al swallowed and nodded. "Yes, sir."

"Good. Dinner is at eight, and I expect you to be there clean, sober, and acting as respectable as you possibly can. But just eat and keep your dirty mouth shut at my table."

"I will do that. Yes, sir. I surely will do that."

Business over, Virden and Seth headed for the door, but after his boss had stepped into the hallway, Seth stopped and said, "Just one more question."

"Why sure!"

"You feel bad about your cousin Carl dyin'?"

Al rubbed his face and stared into those cold fish-eyes. "Seth, we all got to die sooner or later. Reckon it was just poor Carl's time."

"Yeah, reckon it was," came the quiet reply as the door closed and Al sank to his chin in the bathwater.

Chapter 17

They were finishing dinner at the Rimrock Hotel, and it had not been a pleasant experience. The roasted sage grouse was tough and stringy and the potatoes only half-cooked. The only thing that had saved the meal was the large quantity of available wine, which was an outstanding Chablis.

Longarm had been trying to engage the new arrival in conversation, but without much luck. Still, as the dessert arrived, he tried once more. "So, Mr. Hunt, I understand that you have arrived here looking for work."

Al Hunt nodded, remembering the warning that he should try to keep his mouth shut. Still, he couldn't completely ignore a question for a United States marshal, could he?

"That's right, Marshal. Looking for work."

"On the river as a raftsman?"

Hunt glanced at Frankie, who was trying to hide a frown. "Well, Marshal, I'll be an oarsman if that's all that I can find. But I'm not real comfortable on the river. She's a dangerous gal, she is. I'd much rather ride a horse . . . or a woman. . . .no offense, ladies . . . but that's the gawd's truth . . . than a river raft."

"Yes," Longarm said, "I'm sure that is very dangerous work. Have you ever rafted through the entire canyon?"

"No, and I don't expect I ever will."

Hunt sure wished that the marshal would focus his attention on someone else. Frankie Virden stepped in to divert the conversation. "Al is kind of a jack-of-all-trades. He's a good cowboy and mustanger. He's also worked in mines and at logging mills. Isn't that right?"

"Yep."

Longarm turned to the one called Seth. "And you do what?"

"I help Mr. Virden however he needs to be helped."

Longarm studied the man, who was only a couple of years younger than himself. "What's your background?"

"Is this some kind of interrogation?" Seth asked. "What interest could my life be to you?"

"Oh, I think it could be very interesting to me," Longarm said, feeling the tension at the table rising. "I just like to know something about the people that I eat with. That's all."

Seth glanced at his boss, who said, "Seth doesn't like to talk about himself, but I don't think he'd mind if I told you that he came from Virginia City, Nevada, where he was in the saloon business."

"Is that right," Longarm said, tasting his apple pie and finding it to be better than expected. "I've been on the Comstock Lode a few times. Where did you work?"

"Bucket of Blood Saloon and the Silver Dollar."

"Ah, yes. What a view out the back window of the Bucket of Blood."

"It is if you like to look at cemeteries" was Seth's cryptic reply.

"Virginia City is a wild mining town, although the boom has already come and gone."

"Not completely," Seth countered. "They're still finding bodies of pure silver down deep under the town. The Ophir Mine and the Consolidated are still in business."

Longarm nodded, satisfied that Seth was at least telling the truth about where he'd come from. "Were you a bartender at those big saloons?"

"I did whatever was needed, but mostly I was a bouncer."

Seth was of average size and well built but didn't fit the mold of a large and very physical bouncer. Former bouncers Longarm had known had fist-busted noses, and their hands were generally flat-knuckled, but Seth's hands were almost delicate and his nose was thin and straight.

"So," Frankie Virden said before Longarm could ask another question, "I suppose you and your wife will be leaving tomorrow for Lees Ferry and that murder investigation?"

"That's right. Do you know anything about it?"

Virden shook his head. "Miss Blue and I came in from Flagstaff on the same stage with you. Remember?"

"Of course I remember. But you've been up here at your hotel off and on for months. I just thought you might have had a guest passing through who had some information that I'd find helpful . . . or that you and Miss Blue had been to Lees Ferry yourselves and heard all about those prominent missing tourists or the murders."

"No, afraid not, Marshal," Virden said, reaching for a cigar. "But I'm sure you'll find out everything you need to know when you get there tomorrow afternoon. Are you feeling stronger?"

"Strong enough," Longarm replied. He looked across the table at Al Hunt. "But like you, Al, I sure don't want to go down that mighty river and over all those rapids."

Hunt managed a smile and concentrated on his dessert. There was a maid that worked part-time in the kitchen, and although she was older and quite heavy, with a big mole on her chin that sprouted black hairs, he'd charmed her into bringing him a little something to drink in his room after dinner, and he was sure he could mount her for an extra dollar. The thing of it was that it was hard to think of mounting Shirley when right at this table sat two much younger and more beautiful women. But he still had hopes of getting between the legs of the marshal's wife, and there was always Carrie Blue to think about.

"Well," Carrie said, standing with a yawn, "I'm going to turn in for the night. It's been a long day."

"So early, my dear?" Virden asked with surprise.

"Yes, I'm really tired."

"Very well. I'll be along later. I might be able to work up a poker game with Mr. Potter and Marshal Long this evening."

"Not me," Potter said quickly. "We'll be joining the marshal and his wife on their way down to Lees Ferry tomorrow. Going to be quite the experience, and we'll need to be at our best."

"I understand," Virden said. "And what about you, Marshal?"

"I'm not up to a game of cards tonight. Maybe on the way out of the canyon, when we make our return visit."

"Very well. Seth?"

"Sure," Seth told his boss. "I'm in."

"I'll play a hand or two," Al Hunt offered.

"Three it is then," Virden said, not revealing his disappointment until after his guests had excused themselves and gone to their rooms for the night.

"How'd I do?" Al Hunt asked when the three of them were alone.

"You did the best that you could. The marshal seemed especially interested in you, and I wonder if he suspects you might have been in on the ambush."

"Not a chance!" Hunt said quickly. "And what does it matter when he's going to be dead not long after midnight?"

"It doesn't, I suppose."

Hunt said, "I've been sleeping on the ground for the last few days, and I think I'll go to bed now on a real mattress . . . if it's all right with you, sir."

Frankie Virden nodded. "Just don't mess this up tonight. If you do . . . well, I think you know what will happen."

Hunter gulped. "Yes, sir. Don't worry. I'll put a blade through the marshal's gawdamn brisket. And I'll just knock the woman out wearing a mask. It's as good as done, Mr. Virden."

"I hope so for *both* our sakes," Frankie Virden replied.

Fifteen minutes later, Shirley knocked softly on Al Hunt's door then tiptoed quietly into his room. She really was an ugly old horse, but she had a bottle in her hand, so Al didn't care.

He reached for the bottle, but Shirley was quicker than expected and pulled back. "That'll be two dollars, Al."

He grumbled at the price but paid her. "Want to have a drink with me?"

"I really should get back to the kitchen," Shirley told him. "But I wouldn't mind a quick drink."

"How about something *else* quick?" Al asked, taking a long pull on the bottle.

Shirley was missing all her upper front teeth so that when she giggled, she made a sound not unlike that of a kettle on the boil. "And what did you have in mind?"

"One dollar for one big poke in your ass," Al said. "And I ain't in the mood for dickering."

"Two dollars and you can poke it in *all* my holes," she said, grabbing the bottle out of his hands and taking a long pull. "What's it to be?"

Al Hunt clucked his tongue and turned down the light. He unbuttoned his pants, pulled out his manhood, and said, "All right, you fat old pile, get down on your knees and earn your money."

Shirley dropped down on her knees with such force that the floorboards shook under Al's bare feet. But she knew what she was doing, and as Al stood wide-legged, it seemed that the gap in her mouth caused by all those missing teeth made things pretty interesting. Al had planned to take her in the ass next, but Shirley was so surprisingly good on her knees that he grabbed her head and lost his seed in a hot, humping rush.

"Worth it?" she asked, laboring to stand and spitting into his chamber pot.

"Yeah, it was worth it."

"I'll be in the kitchen until midnight if you want seconds, honey."

"Get out of here."

"Then maybe tomorrow?"

"Maybe," Al heard himself say as he ushered her out into the lamplit hallway.

It was after midnight. Shirley was long gone and so was most of the whiskey she'd spirited into his room, but Al wasn't worrying. He lay on his bed staring up at the ceiling with a smile plastered on his face. The candlelight did a shadowy dance over his head, and he felt good and ready for what was next. Frankie had given him a large and very sharp butcher knife from the hotel's kitchen, and he had a mask that would hide his identity. Now all that was left was to kill the bottle and then go down and finish the job that he and poor cousin Carl had botched.

Come morning, he'd be sleeping in, but all hell would be going on elsewhere inside the Rimrock Hotel when people discovered that the rich woman had been beaten into unconsciousness and that the federal marshal was sprouting a large knife from the middle of his chest.

Chapter 18

Heidi and Longarm lay side by side in their hotel room bed, and although Longarm had been weakened, he was not without desire.

"Are you sure?" Heidi whispered.

"Positive."

"All right, but you need your rest, and with your wound I think that I'll do the physical part."

"It's *all* physical."

Heidi laughed and then slid down to take Longarm's manhood in her mouth. In only a few moments, he was standing tall and stiff as a spike.

"Well," she said, climbing onto him. "We'll just do this nice and easy."

"No, we won't," he countered, pulling her down and kissing her mouth. "We'll do it as good as we always do."

Heidi began to move up and down on Longarm, and soon they were lost in their passion, each striving for the sublime moment when they would suddenly be caught up in wildness and ecstasy.

And just as they neared that lofty, lusty pinnacle of

passion, Longarm heard the sound of a key in his door's lock and then a faint squeak as it was being pushed open. In a rush, he emptied his seed, as a dark and crouched form entered the room. Heidi began to cry out with pleasure as Longarm heaved her body off of his own, snatched the pistol at his bedside, and fired as the intruder lunged at him with an upraised knife.

Heidi screamed, probably not because of a sexual climax, but out of shock and surprise. The attacker screamed and crashed facedown on the bed, but Longarm was already rolling onto the floor.

"Holy shit!" Heidi yelled, struggling to get out from under Longarm. "What happened!"

"Some asshole with a big knife just tried to kill us," Longarm said, climbing off his naked companion and then standing over the body on the bed. "And I think we're going to have to have the bedsheets changed right away."

Heidi scrambled erect, heavy breasts wet with perspiration and chest heaving from way too much excitement. "What . . ."

"It's that man, Al Hunt," Longarm told her as he tore the attacker's mask from his face then turned back to Heidi. "Are you all right?"

There was just enough moonlight coming through the curtain for him to see that she was *not* all right. Her bare legs were shaking and her mouth was hanging open as she struggled for her breath.

"What did he do that for!"

"I'm not sure," Longarm replied. "But I expect this room will be full of people in about thirty more seconds, so you might want to get dressed."

"You're the one that's standing there naked and stiff. Maybe you ought to take your own damned advice!"

"Yeah, I guess you're right," he said agreeably.

Longarm placed his gun back on the bedside table and in some pain pulled on his pants and shrugged into a shirt. "Here they come," he said, picking the gun back up because he was still uncertain about what this attempted murder was all about.

Frankie Virden and Seth burst into the room with pistols clenched in their fists.

"Don't shoot," Longarm warned, cocking back the hammer of his six-gun. "The excitement is over for tonight."

Frankie had matches, and when he lit one, the room suddenly revealed the shocking sight of Al Hunt lying facedown on the bed with a red stain rapidly spreading on the sheets.

"It's a bloody mess and we'll need another room for the rest of this night," Longarm told the man.

"What the hell is going on!" Virden shouted.

Longarm's gun was pointed at the gambler and hotel owner. "I think *you* might have the answer to your own question."

"What!"

"You heard me. I can't yet prove it, but I suspect that you knew Hunt was coming in here to stab us to death and then rob us."

"Are you insane!" Virden cried with feigned outrage. "This is *my hotel*. Why the hell would I want someone to be murdered here? Do you have any idea what this will do for my hotel business!"

"I don't know and I don't care. All I'm sure of is that our room was locked and Hunt had a key."

"Then he stole it from behind the desk. All the keys are right out there hanging on a peg."

"I'd suggest you change that," Longarm snapped.

"And if I find anything to tie you into his second attempt in less than five days to kill me, then I'll make sure you hang. You too, Seth."

"Fuck off, Marshal. I don't know anything about this and neither does the boss. Hunt was a crazy bastard who thought he could rob you both, and he made a big mistake."

"Yeah," Longarm said, "he did. Now both of you get out of this room while my wife and I get fully dressed and I see if Hunt has anything I need to know about in his pockets."

Virden swore viciously then said, "I knew that I shouldn't have let that man stay at my hotel. I'll admit that I'm partly to blame for this, but I had no idea that—"

"Stow it," Longarm said impatiently. "Just close the door on your way out."

"But . . ."

"I'll join you in a few minutes and pick up that new room key," Longarm told the pair. He consulted his pocket watch. "Still enough time to get some sleep before a long day tomorrow."

Elmer Potter, wearing a long nightshirt and with his eyes wide and staring pushed through the doorway. "My god!" he cried. "What happened! That man is . . . is dead."

"Go back to your room, Mr. Potter," Longarm commanded. "We've a long day ahead tomorrow and you and your wife need your sleep."

"Sleep?" Potter couldn't seem to tear his eyes off the dead man sprawled in a spreading pool of blood. "How can we sleep when a man just got shot to death not twenty feet from our room!"

Longarm didn't have an answer to that, but Frankie Virden shoved the older man into the hallway. "Marshal,

I'll be waiting in the lobby when you're finished here," he said gravely.

"Yeah."

When they were alone, Heidi collapsed in the chair and buried her head in her hands. She was trembling, and when Longarm tried to console her, she sobbed, "I'm not sure that I'm up to all this killing that seems to follow you around, Custis!"

"I wanted you to stay in Flagstaff and wait for me. Remember?"

"I remember."

"But you wouldn't do it. Would you like to return to Flagstaff when John Wallace comes back?"

"I think I would," she replied. "I . . . I don't want to leave you, but I've seen more bloodshed since we left on that stagecoach than I've seen in my entire life."

"I'm sorry. And do you know what the worst of it is?"

"There's *worse*!"

"Yes," he admitted. "I have a feeling there is much worse to come down at Lees Ferry and on the Colorado River."

"I really miss Denver," she whispered, starting to cry. "I really do."

"Then take the first train back," he urged.

"But what about us? What about . . ."

Longarm knelt in front of the woman, who was fighting off hysteria. "Heidi, there's nothing wrong with being scared and wanting some peace and safety in your life. Nothing wrong at all."

"I'm ashamed of myself for admitting that I just want to leave."

"Don't be," he told her. "I'll return to Denver, and when I do, I'll look you up. I think you should take that job offer and then start your own jewelry business."

"You do?"

"Uh-huh. You'd be amazingly successful."

"But what about *us*!"

"We can talk about us when I return."

"*If* you return. Custis, why can't you and I just leave and go back to Colorado? There must be others who can do this bloody work. We could get married and live—"

Longarm placed a finger over her lips. "This isn't the time to be talking about that. I came to do a job and I'm staying until it's finished."

"Do you think that man lying on our bed is tied to anything else or that he just saw my jewelry and figured he could rob and kill us?"

"I don't have the answer to that . . . yet. But if I had to answer your question based on my instincts and past experience, I'd say that Al Hunt wasn't acting alone and that he might be the ambusher that got away."

"I wonder."

"I'll search him and his room," Longarm told her. "There may be some clues that tie the man to either the ambush or to Frankie Virden. I'll just have to see how that plays out."

"All right."

"Heidi, just pack your things and I'll go get a new room," he said, standing up and tucking his shirt into his pants, then reaching for his socks and boots. "We both need to get some sleep before I leave in the morning."

She nodded and began moving. That was good because packing her things in a bag, getting fully dressed, just going through the motions, might keep her mind off the dead man that lay sprawled out on their bed with a long hunting knife still clenched in his lifeless fist.

Longarm was in a bad and dangerous mood when he

picked up another room key. "I'm going to tell you something, Frankie, just so we understand each other."

"And that would be?"

"It's obvious that Al Hunt would have had easy access to the spare key to our room . . . but what is less obvious to me is why you or someone at the desk didn't notice the key was missing."

Frankie Virden managed a smile. "Al Hunt must have grabbed it off the hook after we all had dinner. We were very busy and apparently no one noticed that your spare room key was missing."

"I see."

"An unfortunate mistake," Virden assured him. "I should never have allowed a man like Hunt to stay in this hotel. Word of his attempt on your life will certainly filter back to Flagstaff and hurt my hotel business."

"How sad," Longarm said without sympathy.

"Yes, it is sad. But at least you and Mrs. Long are unharmed and Hunt is dead. I say good riddance to the man."

Longarm had a strong suspicion that Frankie Virden and Seth had given Al Hunt the key to his room after dinner, but that couldn't be proved, so he said, "Make sure that those keys aren't sitting out in the open when my wife and I get up in the morning."

"Is that an *order*, Marshal?"

"Yeah, it is," Longarm said, marching off to open up the new room.

"Marshal?"

Longarm turned in the dim hallway to see Carrie Blue standing in her nightgown. "What is it?"

"I just wanted to tell you that Al Hunt and Carl Whitfield were cousins."

"Is that a fact!"

"Yes."

"Do you know if Frankie and Seth were in on the attempt just made on my life and that of my wife?"

"I . . . I couldn't say. All I can tell you is that they were all together talking around the poker table last evening in low voices."

"Thank you for telling me this," Longarm said. "Now, you'd better get back to your bed. I assume that Frankie would not be pleased if he caught you with me."

"No, he wouldn't."

Longarm squeezed her arm. "You're better than this, Carrie."

"That's what Mr. Wallace says. He's going to help me find some honest work in Flagstaff and take me back with him when he returns on his stagecoach."

"What will Frankie do?"

"I don't know. I'm . . . I'm terrified that he or Seth will kill Mr. Wallace."

"Let me think about this," Longarm told her. "Now, go back to your room."

Carrie looked as if she was about to burst into tears, but she left anyway. Longarm did a quick inspection of their replacement room and then he went back to the original room and got Heidi. He took her to their new room and said, "Lock the door and I'll be back in ten minutes or less."

"But where are you going!"

"I'm going to search Al Hunt's body and see if it turns up anything of interest."

Heidi looked pale and scared, but she did as he asked. Ten minutes later, Longarm had finished his examination of the body and found nothing remarkable. But he was still thinking about what Carrie Blue had told him.

And, even more important, the sobering fact that neither Frankie Virden nor Seth had told him that Al Hunt had been Carl Whitfield's cousin. To Longarm's way of thinking, it was as good as proof that they were the two men who had ambushed him after he left the Cameron Trading Post.

Chapter 19

Longarm and the older couple, Mr. and Mrs. Potter, were packed and anxious to leave the Rimrock Hotel the next day at noon on rented horses. The Potters appeared to have aged considerably since the attempt on Longarm's life shortly after midnight. Longarm had said his good-bye to Heidi and she was still sleeping. In another day or two, she'd return to Flagstaff with John Wallace and Carrie Blue.

"I can't wait to get leave of this place," Mrs. Potter confided. "There is something very evil here, and Elmer and I have decided we will not be staying at this hotel after we've seen Lees Ferry and the Grand Canyon."

"Where will you go?"

"We're not sure yet," the older woman confided. "But we certainly don't feel safe here!"

Longarm happened to get a fleeting glimpse of Carrie Blue out of the corner of his eye. She had been peering through the window of her hotel room, and there was something about her expression and looks that stopped him in his tracks.

"We'll be looking forward to your return," Virden was saying. "Marshal, be careful down there in the canyon. And I hope you find out what happened to those people that went missing."

Carrie Blue suddenly bent her head, cupped her face in her hands, and disappeared from Longarm's sight.

"Hold on just a minute," Longarm said, turning and marching back into the hotel.

"Hey!" Frankie Virden called. "What . . ."

But Longarm wasn't listening to the man as he strode through the lobby and down a hallway to Frankie Virden's room. And he didn't listen when Carrie cried out for him to go away and leave her alone. Instead, Longarm opened the door and stepped into the room and then he came to an abrupt stop.

"Carrie! What happened!"

Her beautiful face had been viciously battered. The former black eye that she'd been trying to hide was now swollen completely shut and her lips were puffy and crusted with dried blood.

Longarm closed the door behind him and approached the cringing young woman. "Did Frankie do this last night after you told me about Al Hunt and Carl Whitfield being cousins?"

"Yes, and Seth," she managed to say. "But . . ."

Longarm collected the frightened young woman into his arms. "He isn't going to hurt you ever again. And neither is Seth. I can promise you that much."

"Not even you can help me out here, and when you leave . . ."

"I can't leave you or Heidi alone with that pair. Not for one single hour."

The door burst open, and both Virden and Seth bulled their way inside the room. Frankie was in the front and blocking the doorway, "What is going on!"

"That's what I was going to ask you," Longarm said, his rage bubbling so near the surface that he was ready to explode. "Miss Blue says that you both had a turn at her last night after she and I talked in the hallway."

"She's lying."

"Carrie is telling the truth, and I'm convinced that you both sent Al Hunt into my room last night to stab me to death while I was asleep."

"You can't prove that!" Virden shouted.

"His knife came out of your kitchen." Longarm glanced to Carrie. "I'm sure she'll recognize it, won't you, Carrie?"

She managed to whisper. "They put Al up to stabbing you to death and then they planned to steal—"

"The whoring bitch is lying!" Seth bellowed.

"No, she isn't, and both you and Frankie are going to prison. I think you'll find that the Yuma Territorial Prison is the closest thing to hell you can find on earth."

Both men were armed, but it was Seth who started the play by clawing for his holstered pistol. Trouble was, Frankie was blocking his line of fire.

Longarm's hand shot across his belt buckle and tore his own gun out of his holster. He fired in one smooth, practiced motion. His first bullet caught Frankie as the man was going for a derringer in his vest pocket. Frankie's body slammed back into Seth, whose aim was knocked off target. A bullet from Seth's gun cut through Frankie's knee and then Longarm was emptying his gun as both men were knocked backward into the hallway in a shower of bright red blood.

*   *   *

The next afternoon Longarm, Heidi, and Carrie stood apart from the heavyset Shirley. Two stoic men who had been on Frankie's payroll finished digging three graves not fifty yards from the rim of the Grand Canyon. Longarm had thought about having the bodies returned to Flagstaff for a proper burial, but the Arizona afternoon temperature was very warm and the corpses would have been badly decayed by the time they were delivered to a mortuary.

"Drop them into the holes and cover them up," Longarm ordered.

When the bodies were covered, Longarm asked, "Anyone here care to say a few words of forgiveness?"

No one cared to say a few words, but one of the sweating workmen muttered, "At least they'll have a view of the canyon."

"Not from five feet under," Longarm said.

"What about the hotel?" the other workman asked. "Frankie didn't have any relatives."

"Then it belongs to his fiancée."

"Miss Carrie Blue?"

"That's right. When a man without any relatives is engaged, the law says that everything he owns goes to his fiancée."

Both Carrie and Heidi looked over at him, but neither one said a word. Longarm had made that up, but he figured he would find a way to make it stick so that Carrie Blue . . . and maybe John Wallace . . . would assume ownership of the hotel. Things like this happened all the time, and if anyone had earned the hotel and a chance for a new life and hope, it was Miss Carrie Blue.

"When John Wallace arrives with his stage, tell him

what I said and that Heidi is going back to Flagstaff on his stagecoach."

"I've changed my mind," she said. "I've decided to stay right here until you come back from inside the canyon. Carrie and I can handle this place until you return. The Potters have decided to stay and catch the first stagecoach back to Flagstaff."

"Long way for them to come and not actually go down into the Grand Canyon."

"They said they've seen enough of it already," Heidi told him. "We all have."

"Are you sure?" Longarm asked.

"Positive," Heidi replied. "But I'll be here when you return."

Longarm couldn't help but smile. "In that case, I'll be taking one of the horses and getting along down to Lees Ferry."

He didn't bother watching as the last shovelfuls were tossed on the three graves. Frankie, Seth, and Al Hunt had been rotten to the core, and he suspected that they'd probably conspired to kill more than one unsuspecting sightseer for their money and jewelry. The single, fatal mistake they'd made that had put an end to their scheming and deadly ways was that they should have stuck with robbing and killing tourists instead of a United States marshal.

Chapter 20

Longarm bought a jug-headed roan gelding for thirteen dollars and a battered saddle for four, and a few more government dollars got him a bridle, blankets, saddle-bags, provisions, and five pounds of grain to keep Old Red moving and upright.

"Are you *sure* this horse will get me all the way down to Lees Ferry?" he asked the grizzled prospector and hunter who wandered along the south rim looking for gold and collecting hides and horns. "He looks like he's about ready to fall over and die."

"Aw, don't you worry, Marshal! Old Red is a fine horse, and he's good for another five years at least."

The roan was mangy and underweight, and his head was larger than most lady's suitcases. "How old is he?"

The man threw up his hands and shook them at the clear blue sky. "I ain't gonna tell you no lies, Marshal. Fact is, I don't know how old he is. Not as old as me, because he's a smooth mouth and . . ."

"He's nearly lost all his teeth! Isn't there a better horse around here I can buy?"

"Nope. Mr. John Wallace told me that you gave his favorite buckskin mare away to a Navajo. I wouldn't sell an Indian a good horse."

"The Navajo kid and his family saved my life! It's the least they deserved."

The man scratched his bearded face and shook his head. "You might just see it that way, but I surely don't. So do you want to buy Old Red . . . or not?"

"I'll buy him, but if he doesn't get me down to Lees Ferry and back I want a damned refund."

"No, sir! Once you buy a horse . . . he's yours. That's the way we look at it in these parts."

The buckskin-clad hunter and prospector smiled to reveal that, like his horse, he was almost toothless. "Tell you what, Marshal, it's only about forty miles down to Lees Ferry. Might be you'd like to hike it down and back. Course, comin' out of the canyon can be a little tiring, but . . ."

"Sold," Longarm growled and reached for his wallet.

In a half hour he was ready to ride. Heidi gave him a kiss and hug, then Carrie Blue did the same. "Marshal Long," Carrie said, "I don't know how to thank you for what you did for me . . . and all of us."

"Frankie, Seth, and Al Hunt were filled with bad intentions," Longarm told the two women. "I did the Arizona Territory a big favor and saved the taxpayers money by not having them take up jail or court time."

"But," Carrie said, "I mean about the hotel and what you said about me ownin' it."

"Do you know if Frankie ever even recorded a deed at the county courthouse for the ownership of this property?"

"I don't believe that he did," Carrie said. "Frankie just sort of took what he wanted and then did things legal-like only if he was forced to do them."

"Then if I were you," Longarm suggested, "I'd see if I could buy a legal claim to this hotel and the land it sets upon."

"I don't have any money. Well, only a hundred dollars or so, and that sure won't buy me either the land or the hotel that it sits upon."

"Maybe," Longarm said, looking at Heidi, "you can find an investor either in Heidi or even John Wallace. Think that might be possible?"

Heidi nodded.

Carrie Blue giggled. "I think it might be! John needs this hotel to have a place to take his stagecoach passengers, and he told me before he went back to Flagstaff this last time that he wished like anything he could have talked Frankie into selling it to him."

"Well there you go," Longarm said.

"Be careful," Heidi pleaded, looking up at Longarm. "Just come back alive and ready to join me on the train back to Denver."

"That is my full and sincere intention," Longarm assured the beautiful woman. He grabbed the saddle horn. "Brace yourself, Red!"

When Longarm jammed his foot into the stirrup, the roan gelding sort of widened his stance and stiffened all fours. When Longarm mounted, the horse wobbled for an instant, then turned its big head around to gaze at Longarm with a big eyeball.

"So long," Longarm told the women. "You too, Mr. and Mrs. Potter!"

The couple waved, and Longarm nudged the gelding with his boot heels. Old Red lurched forward and started moving about as fast as frozen molasses coming out of a jar.

Longarm banged his heels against the animal's rib

cage. "Come on, Red! If you don't walk any faster than that, winter will catch us before we get to the bottom of the Grand Canyon!"

Old Red picked up the pace a little, and Longarm twisted around in his sorry saddle and waved the women and everyone else good-bye. He saw that someone had put little wooden crosses over the three fresh graves. Nice gesture, but Longarm didn't think it was appropriate given that those three were probably already roasting in hell.

It took him the best part of a full day to reach the bottom of the Grand Canyon and then get a Mormon to ferry him across the Colorado River. Down inside the Canyon the air was hot and humid and the roar of the river was overpowering and constant. Red and pale brown layers of ancient and broken rock climbed like a giant staircase everywhere you looked. The Colorado River was running low after the heavy spring flooding that had left drift-wood and marks twenty feet up on the walls, but even so the water was way too deep to swim a horse across, even a young one. Longarm reckoned that Old Red most likely wouldn't have gotten halfway across before giving up and sinking like a stone.

"How are you doin' today!" the burly young man who skillfully guided the big raft across the river shouted.

"I'm doin' fine."

"Here for the fishin'?"

"Nope."

"Gonna ride the rapids, are you?"

"Not unless I have to." Longarm clung to a rope affixed to a stanchion bolted to the raft. Old Red snorted and stomped, looking uneasily at the brown, roiling water.

"Water always this muddy?" Longarm called to the young man, who was working a big single oar off the back of the raft.

"Yep! I've heard some say it's muddier than the Ole Mississippi, but I never seen the Mississippi, so I couldn't tell you if that was true."

"It's true," Longarm shouted over the river's thunder.

The young man was working hard, and as the raft made its way at an angle across the current, Longarm could see that it was going to beach right at a dirt track that led down from between a tall, red-stone canyon.

When the raft grated against the gravel and sand, shuddering to a stop, Old Red showed more life than usual and stampeded off onto solid ground. Longarm damn near lost control of the horse, but he doubted the roan would have run any farther than the first patch of grass.

"Not much of a horse you got there, mister. On an old horse like that you might have a hard time getting back out of this big canyon."

"I expect he will surprise all of us and climb out like a mountain goat," Longarm replied, tightening his cinch and swinging up into the saddle. "I'm looking for the raft company where I understand some people were murdered a few weeks ago."

The young man blinked and shaded his eyes as he stared up at Longarm. "You're a lawman, I expect."

"That's right."

"Thought you were from the first moment I laid eyes on you ridin' down from the other side. Where you from?"

"Denver."

The big, sandy-haired kid smiled. "I heard it's a nice town. The biggest I ever seen was Salt Lake City. Went up to see a girl named Sarah, but she'd already been married off to an elder about twice her age. I'm still a bachelor, but they'll find me a suitable wife before much longer, and I hope she ain't real ugly or fat. I'm only twenty and I'd like to be a farmer someday, but I'll never be able to afford the land and machinery it takes to work a place. No farm, no wife, no future for me, I'm afraid."

Longarm formed an instant liking for the strong young lad. He had a full beard and his forearms were corded with muscle and his legs were like tree stumps. "You live here at Lees Ferry?"

"Nope. I live in a cabin little ways upriver. Live by myself without as much as a dog. In the spring, this ferry crossing is mighty busy and the river is high and most dangerous. I've been workin' here two years and only lost one wagon and team."

"Any people?"

The young man's blue eyes fell and his smile died. "I was just a helper learnin' this job when the raft flipped and we lost six . . . two parents and four kids. It was a mighty sad time for a while."

"I need to find out what has been going wrong down here," Longarm said, deciding to confide in the young man.

"Meanin' you'd be lookin' for Judge Milton Quinn and his young wife."

"That's right. Have they shown up?"

"Nope. Not alive or dead. They're still just missin', and I believe they've long since fed themselves to the fish."

"Who should I talk to about all this?" Longarm asked, paying an extra dollar for the information.

The young man pointed downriver. "There's a cabin, lodging, place to buy food and supplies . . . It's a store, with little shacks for sleepin' in, but the prices are mighty high. They run rafting trips out of a cove right there and horseback rides for tourists up into the canyons and other places."

"I see."

"My name is Jacob Young."

"Any relation to your prophet Brigham Young?"

The young man laughed. "Half of our community are related in some way to the prophet. Me, I'm so distantly related that they hardly know I exist except in the big books at the temple."

"Well, my name is Marshal Custis Long and I appreciate the information you've given me."

"You just watch yourself, Marshal. Those people down there where I told you are a den of thieves and cut-throats. They're only in it for the money. Godless people and worse."

"Thanks for the warning."

"Anyone in these parts would freely give you the same warning."

"If these people are so . . . so mean and moneygrubbing, how come a man as important as Judge Quinn and his young wife would come and have anything to do with them?"

Jacob Young shook his head. "There are those who won't have anything to do with us Mormon folks. No sir, they'd rather consort with thieves, liars, drunks, whores, and Satan-lovers than deal with us."

"And that's why Judge Quinn and his wife went to these people?"

Jacob shrugged his broad shoulders. "You'd have to ask them about that . . . but most likely it's too late to ask them about anything. Mostly, Marshal, I'm just being an honest and God-fearin' man who is trying to warn you that those people won't respect you or your badge. You go among the godless and they'll show you no quarter, federal officer or not."

Longarm thanked the young Mormon again and rode on down the trail. He came to a fork where one track led up into the canyon where he'd been told the Lee Family still lived, but he took the other fork in the road, the one that followed the big, muddy river west, deeper and deeper into the mighty Grand Canyon. The walls were closing in hard over him and the sun was gone, leaving him in shadow. But even in shadow the air was stifling and hot. And try as he might, Longarm couldn't shake a bad feeling that he was riding into something both sinister and deadly.

Chapter 21

Longarm was looking hot and ragged by the time he rode up to the shanty with the sign that read: BOAT TRIPS AND HORSEBACK RIDES. HUNTERS AND TOURISTS WELCOME.

He took one look at the run-down operation and the herd of skinny, mangy ponies corralled nearby, the sagging and dirty tents for rent and the storefront and saloon, and reckoned the whole outfit couldn't represent an investment of more than a hundred dollars.

Two tall and ragged-looking men were sitting in rickety chairs in front of the store and saloon, and they offered little greeting when Longarm rode up and dismounted.

"Afternoon," Longarm said to the pair. "Can a man get a drink and a meal here?"

"A man that has money can get most anything he wants right here," the taller of the two replied after spitting a stream of tobacco into the dirt. "You got some money, mister?"

"I have a little, yes. Not that it's any of your damned business."

"Don't need to get uppity on us," the other man said. "It's just that we deal in cash and gold. You ain't got either, then you'd best move along."

Longarm had the feeling that this pair was not overly bright and that they were also not in charge. He tied Old Red to a hitching rail and walked past the two men without another word. When he got inside the hot, crowded store, he found a plank stretched across two empty whiskey barrels and behind it a big woman with a dirty rag wrapped around her head and a pistol strapped to her ample waist. She might have been thirty, but she looked far older.

"Any whiskey left that's drinkable?" he asked.

The woman was just as unfriendly as the pair outside. "Any cash in your pockets, mister?"

Longarm laid a silver dollar on the plank. "That ought to buy me a couple drinks and a good meal."

"Maybe in Flagstaff or on the reservation it would, but everything we have has to be freighted a long damn way down here. So your dollar will get you two drinks and a plate of cold beef and beans."

"Then that's what I'll have," Longarm told the woman. "Whiskey first."

What she poured was so murky you couldn't see through it from one side of the glass to the other. When Longarm raised the glass to his lips, it even smelled bad. "What kind of horse piss do you serve here?"

"One kind and you're holdin' it," she snapped, taking the dollar and dropping it into her dirty dress pocket. "You want that plate of beef and beans now?"

"If it is fit to eat."

"It's fit. Maybe you'd like to get fancy and buy a can of peaches to go with it," she suggested.

Longarm shook his head and choked down the

whiskey in a single gulp. "Worst horse piss I've had in a long, long time. Got any beer?"

"Nope."

"Then give me another glass and bring that food along."

The woman squinted one eye, spat her own stream of tobacco on the floor, and growled, "You're kinda used to givin' folks orders, huh?"

"I am as a matter of fact."

"Well," she said, lips curling down at the corners, "down here in the canyon we don't cotton to strangers who are uppity and like to give orders."

Longarm took a step back. "Are you and those two half-wits outside completely stupid or are you three just plain disagreeable and ornery?"

"Mister, I'm ornery enough to tell you to eat your meal, drink your second drink, and then drag your tall ass back to wherever it came from!"

Longarm had rarely seen such open hostility . . . especially from someone who ought to be trying to make money off the sale of food or drinks. He wanted to let these ignorant people know that he wasn't in any mood for their orneriness. He also wanted to tell them that he was a federal marshal that had come a long way to learn about the disappearances of a judge and his wife and also the death of three river guides, but he decided to hold his silence for the time being.

"Here," the woman said, slapping a jug on the plank. "Pour yourself another glass and try to be more sociable, or leave . . . makes no matter to me."

Longarm poured. The woman went into another small room and came back a few minutes later with a bent tin plate filled with some greasy beef and cold beans. "You can eat right there on the bar."

"You call this rotting plank a 'bar'?"

"It serves the purpose of one."

Longarm lifted the plate and took a good smell. It didn't stink, and he guessed it wasn't rotten, so he demanded a knife and spoon, which seemed to nettle the ugly woman no end.

"Most folks eat it with their fingers," she snorted, disappearing for a moment to return with a knife and fork. "But then some can't wipe their asses properly, so I guess they need a knife and a fork."

Longarm bit back a reply and cut the lardy beef and chomped it down. He hadn't eaten much since leaving the Rimrock Hotel, and he was famished enough to endure this cold and miserable meal.

"I was thinking of renting a boat and riding the river a ways," he said after he'd managed to swallow his food and then toss down the cloudy whiskey. "I saw those boats beached on the sand and figured that they were for rent."

"Ha!" The woman put her hands on her hips and gave him a superior smile. "You ain't no riverboat man! Why, if you got out on that Colorado River, it'd sweep you away and drown your ass at the first little rapids and white water. Not that I'd give a damn . . . but them boats are too good to lose."

"So I have to hire one or both of those morons out front to take me on the river?"

"That's the size of it." She cackled. "But if you want to take a bath in the river, be our guest! Course, it's even dirtier than yourself."

Longarm burped, and the aftertaste in his mouth wasn't pleasant. "What's your name?"

"Gertie. Gertie Rowe. What's it to you?"

"Are those two inbred-looking fellas outside your brothers?"

"Matter of fact they are. Wade and Orvis Rowe. And now that I've told you that, what's your gawdamn handle?"

"Custis Long."

"Well," she said, looking him up and down. "You're long, all right. Taller than Wade or Orvis, I'd say. You probably got a longer cock on you too."

"You'll never know," he told her.

"Hump! If you wanted a poke in me, I'd probably turn you down."

"I wouldn't put my cock in you even if someone held a shotgun to my head, Gertie."

"You are an uppity bastard, Custis Long. Do you want to spend the night? I can rent you a tent that'll keep you dry if it rains tonight. Your horse looks like a dyin' bag of bones, and a bag of oats and some cut grass is for sale."

Longarm belched again and felt a little queasy in the stomach. "Tell you what, Gertie. I've had about all the fun and laughter I can stand being here with you. But I will pay you another dollar to hear what you have to say about the disappearance of Judge Quinn and his young wife a few weeks ago, along with how three river guides had their throats slit."

"So *that's* your game! You're a fuckin' lawman!" Gertie cackled and shouted, "Hey, Wade! We got ourselves a lawman come askin' questions about that judge and his pretty little squat! And about them fellas that got drunk a few weeks ago, got fightin' and cut each other's throats!"

Longarm shook his head. "Gertie, are you tryin' to tell me they all cut each other's throats?"

"Why sure! They got drunker than loons right here at this bar, and when they started to quarreling, I threw them out. Next thing I know they are down on the beach around our boats fightin' and howlin' like wild Indians on firewater. Why, me and my brothers just decided to let them have their fight and stay out of it, and the next mornin', when we got up and went down to see 'em, they was all dead as dogs."

"Gertie, I've heard some lame lies in my time, but that one just takes the cake. It really does. Surely you can come up with something better."

"She's tellin' you how it happened, Lawman. Best not be callin' my sister a liar."

Longarm turned around to see the taller of the pair standing with an old Navy Colt pointed at him. "Are you Wade or Orvis?"

The tall man blinked. "Orvis. And I reckon you need to unbuckle that gun and let it drop to the floor."

"Are you three planning on *robbing* me?" Longarm asked with surprise. "I'm a United States marshal, and if you don't put that old Navy away right now I'm going to ram it up your skinny ass and pull the trigger."

"Ha!" Gertie cried, scooping up a shotgun from somewhere behind the bar and cocking back the hammer. "Look at this stupid, uppity lawman! We're holdin' all the cards in this game, and he's threatening' to shove your gun up your ass, Orvis!"

"Maybe that rotgut he just drank already poisoned his brain," Wade chortled.

"Mister Lawman," Orvis said, all humor falling away, "with your left hand and usin' your fingers only, lift that Colt that's facin' butt forward up and then drop it on the floor nice and easy."

"Looks like a good gun," Wade said, "probably worth fifteen, maybe even twenty dollars. And those boots and that hat . . ."

"Shut up," Orvis ordered.

"Only tellin' what I see," Wade whined.

"Mister," Orvis said, "I ain't goin' to ask you a second time to unholster that hog leg and then reach for the sky."

Longarm knew that he had no chance, with Gertie at his back holding a shotgun and the man in front of him holding the Navy, so he did as he was told.

"Now," Orvis said, "get down on your knees."

"I already said my prayers," Longarm told him, forcing a hard smile.

"Well, they ain't bein' answered, Mister Lawman. Now, do it!"

Longarm's mind was racing. How in the world was he going to get out of this mess alive? "One question, if you don't mind. Did the three of you kill the judge and his young wife and dump their bodies in the river?"

"What's it your business to know?" Orvis demanded. "Could be you'll wind up the same way."

"So you *did* murder them both?"

"We murdered the judge, but the woman escaped and jumped into one of our boats to get away clean. She'd have drowned though 'cause she don't know that big river and she didn't look strong enough to handle a pair of oars. But damn she was pretty!"

"Shut up, Wade!" Gertie and Orvis both shouted at the same time.

"Oh," Longarm said, trying hard to sound matter-of-fact, "I was almost certain that you'd robbed and killed the judge and his wife. Glad to hear that the woman got away. And what about the three river guides?"

"What about 'em?"

"Well," Longarm mused, "my guess is that all of you were drunk and one of you geniuses slipped up and admitted to killing the judge and trying to kill his wife. Having done that, you had no choice but to kill those river guides to keep them from telling people your secret."

"I told you they slit each other's damned throats!" Gertie screamed, jabbing the shotgun into Longarm's spine.

Longarm nodded. "With a little help from Wade and Orvis, I'll bet."

"Mister, you are about to meet your maker," Orvis growled. "But before you do, I'd like to know if any more lawmen are comin' our way."

"If I disappear, you can be sure of it," Longarm told them.

"Well, Mister Lawman, you *have* to disappear," Gertie said. "But I'd rather we spilled your blood and guts outside where the varmints will clean it up instead of right here where I'll have to do it."

"Sure," Longarm said cryptically, "why mess up such a nice place as you have here?"

"You've got a smart mouth on you, Marshal," Gertie hissed. "Gonna be a pleasure to toss your dead ass in the river. Boys, he's wearin' a nice watch and chain. I want that when you've taken care of him."

"Enough talk," Longarm said, stepping toward the door. "If I'm going to die, I'd like to get it over with."

"And aren't you the brave one," Wade snarled. "Maybe we'll just shoot some bullets into your balls and let you jump around a little before we put you out of your misery."

Longarm swallowed hard. "You people are real thoughtful. Why don't we get moving, because this hog sty you call a store and saloon is about to make me puke."

"Get him out of here and get it done," Gertie hissed.

Longarm knew that he had one chance and one chance only, and that was when he stepped through the door. If he could step through it and use the double-barreled .44-caliber derringer attached to his watch fob, he could spin and shoot the closest one in the head and use his second shot to kill the other brother. Gertie and her shotgun were going to be tougher to kill because there was no way she could miss him at close range.

One thing for certain, Longarm had no intention of winding up being fish food like the late Judge Quinn and his pretty young wife, Mavis.

Chapter 22

"Just one thing," Longarm said as he walked between Wade and Orvis on his way to the door.

"And what the hell is that?" Wade demanded.

Longarm stepped through the doorway and spun on his heel, hand going for the hide-out derringer he always carried in his vest pocket. "This!"

The derringer had saved his life on many occasions, and now it came out of his pocket with well-practiced ease. The dull-witted Wade had been right behind him, but Longarm's unexpected remark had momentarily distracted him. Longarm didn't even try to aim but shoved the gun into Wade's belly and unleashed his first shot. The retort sounded like the trunk of a big tree snapping in a very high wind.

"Ugggh!" Wade screamed, falling back into Orvis, who was right on his heels. Wade's gun barked, but its bullet struck a porch post. Longarm grabbed the dying man to use as a shield and fired the derringer again almost point-blank into Orvis, who started backpedaling into the store and crashed over a pickle barrel, spilling its brine across the floor to mix with his blood.

"Gawdamn you!" Gertie screamed, rounding the plank bar top with her single-barreled shotgun. "Damn you to hell!"

Longarm's derringer was empty, and he knew he didn't have time to scoop up one of the fallen brother's pistols before Gertie would be hovering over him to unleash a killing blast. There being no alternative, he turned and ran like hell straight for the Colorado River.

Old Red almost jumped right out of his skin when Gertie fired off her porch at the fleeing Longarm. The roan gelding reared back, busting his reins, and went galloping away, showing amazing speed. Longarm felt several shotgun pellets swarm around him, but Gertie was big and slow and he was lean and fast, and he had enough wits about him not to run in a straight line for the nearby river.

Boom!

A second blast resounded up and down the towering canyon walls as Longarm shoved a rowboat into the water and then dove into it as the current began to slowly spin the wooden craft downriver.

Frantic and knowing the crazy woman was coming, Longarm grabbed oars and saw big, fat Gertie lumber to the water's edge and pry an empty shell out of the shotgun and insert a fresh round. Longarm ducked low in the boat as it seemed to take forever to gain momentum.

Boom!

He was almost out of the shotgun's range now, but several pieces of lead cut through the boat's side, sending splinters flying. Gertie was screaming, but her voice was growing fainter as the boat finally began to accelerate with the swift, roiling current. The fat woman was running as fast as she could along the beach while trying to reload. Longarm grabbed the oars and pulled with all his might as he willed the current to take him completely out of her deadly shotgun's range.

If the situation had not been so desperate, Longarm would have howled with laughter watching the fat, ugly Gertie trying to reload and run at the same time. But the hard truth was that Gertie was closing in and would have probably blown both Longarm and his boat to smithereens except that she tripped over a tree root and crashed face-first onto the muddy beach.

"Ha!" Longarm shouted. "Gawdamn you, Gertie! I'll come back and see you hanged with a stout chain, you fat, ugly pig!"

Gertie looked up, her mud-plastered face actually an improvement. She spat mud and jumped up, grabbing the shotgun and trying to get it un-fouled of the mud. But by then Longarm was pulling on the oars and heading for white-water rapids.

"Oh shit," he cried as the shot-riddled rowboat began to take on water and bounce like a cork on a storm-tossed ocean. "Oh, shit!"

The rowboat *was* sinking. The rapids were roaring in his ears and white water was boiling all around him. Longarm was a strong swimmer, but this situation demanded something beyond any mere human's physical capacity.

The rowboat struck a boulder jutting out of the water and its hull splintered. Water squirted along the crack into the boat, and Longarm desperately pulled for the opposite shore as the boat began to spin in lazy, dying circles.

He tore off his coat and boots, knowing they would only drag him down. Longarm went back to the oars, but now it was like trying to move an elephant stuck in quicksand.

He saw another boulder directly up ahead and pulled on the oars with all his might, trying to avoid another collision. The roar of the mighty Colorado filled his ears, and he could barely see for the spray in his face.

Ride this sinking son of a bitch as long as it's afloat, and when it goes under, grab wood and swim for your life, Custis!

That was all he could think of to do now, but given the power that got ahold of him it seemed most likely that he was going to wind up like all the others . . . just more fish food.

Chapter 23

The boat struck the boulder and tried to lift up over the top of it, but that's when the hull broke completely in half. For one terrifying moment, Longarm was airborne. He looked down at the raging river and hoped that he would not fall to be impaled on some sharply pointed rock or piece of hung-up driftwood.

He tumbled back into the water. Its current was so powerful it pulled him deeper, so that his body kept striking submerged rocks.

Longarm fought wildly to reach the surface, although he was not entirely sure which direction that might be. The water was so muddy that he was a blind man clawing at unseen things, smashing into unseen objects and trying to retain his consciousness even as his lungs were screeching for oxygen.

At last! At last his head burst into air and he swung his long arms around until he felt a large piece of the rowboat's hull. Longarm's fingers clamped onto the wood and he hung on tightly as the river bore him over the rapids. His legs were being hammered unmercifully against barely submerged rocks. He couldn't see, sometimes went under for a moment, but then managed to get his head above water again and grab the wooden wreckage.

At last he was through the rapids, and although the river was still hammering his body, the roar lessened somewhat and he could see himself being carried around a sharp bend. The cliffs had already closed in on him, and directly overhead was a bright blue wedge of sky.

Longarm drew a forearm across his face and looked for a beach or cove where he might be able to survive. He saw several places where small side canyons came down to the Colorado from both the north and south rims, but the current was still so fast he wasn't able to reach them.

And then . . . then he saw the big side canyon and a beach with willows and cottonwood trees about a half mile ahead on the south shore. Longarm also heard the already much too familiar sound of roaring water up ahead and knew that he was in for another stretch of rapids, possibly even worse than the ones he'd barely survived.

This is your chance! This is your only chance! Leave this wreckage and swim for your life!

That was what his brain was telling him, and although it was a hard choice to let go of his pitiful flotation, Longarm did so and started swimming with all of his will and might. He kept his head down and swam like any man would swim when his survival depended on it.

And finally, his cupped and churning hands struck the gravel of the shoreline and he dragged his body up on the sand and mud, feeling the warmth of the sun. The Colorado and its submerged rocks had torn most of his clothing away. No coat, shirt, or vest remained on his scratched and bleeding torso. His boots were missing and so was one leg of his trousers. His gunbelt was still strapped around his waist, but he'd had to leave his Colt on the floor of the store and saloon.

He had a pocketknife . . . a good, sharp one. And when he pushed himself up on his hands and knees and crawled farther up onto the shore, he realized that his legs had not been broken, nor were any of his joints dislocated.

Amazing!

And then Longarm saw something even more amazing. A campfire ring of stones. And charred animal bones and even . . . even the rinds of squash!

He shook his soaked head and staggered to his bare feet. Once there had been people here . . . and not so long ago, because the ashes in the ring of stones had not been washed away by summer rains, and the rinds were not so shriveled by the hot sun as to become brown rings.

Longarm cupped his hands to his mouth and in a voice he barely recognized shouted, "Hello! Hello! Anyone still here!"

His cry echoed hollowly against the soaring stone walls and fled down the river, dissolving into nothingness like smoke.

He was alone . . . maybe.

Longarm found a rock and sat down to rest and assess his situation. The mouth of the canyon fed a small stream of pure, clean water to the big muddy river. He had something clean to drink. And maybe he could climb out of the canyon onto the south rim and find help. But what could he eat?

"I'll figure it out as I go," he said to himself as his head tipped back and he stared up the brush-choked canyon, his eyes measuring the height of its sandstone walls. "I'll make it!"

Longarm stood and cast a final glance back at the
Colorado River. He hoped never to see it again, and then
he turned and started walking. There was a game trail
and maybe a human trail leading south and up the
canyon.

"I can make it," he told himself. "I'll get out of here
alive or die trying."

A hundred yards up the trail and right beside the stream
he saw a body, and that brought Longarm running. He
ran even harder when the body moved just slightly.

When he reached the body, he knelt and without really
thinking about it, he said, "You have to be Mrs. Mavis
Quinn."

The woman was very thin and weak. Her lips were
cracked and her face was burned by wind and sun, but
she was conscious, and when she gripped his hand, she
whispered, "I knew someone would come to find me.
Who are you?"

"United States Marshal Custis Long, at your service."

Her hand gripped his wrist tightly. "Do you have any
food?"

"No," he had to admit. "But I'll find some for us."

"I ate every bit of the Indians' squash . . . a long time
ago it seems. The squash wasn't ripe and I got sick. I
stoned a pink rattlesnake and tried to eat its raw flesh.
Do you see it?"

Now Longarm noticed the dead snake, and it really
was pink. "Doesn't look too appetizing, but it probably
tasted better than my last meal."

It was a joke that fell flat.

"I'm starving, Marshal. My husband was murdered
and . . ."

He placed a hand gently over her lips. "I know all about that. Just rest easy and I'll find something to eat."

"Please find something better than that awful rattlesnake."

"I'll do my best, Mrs. Quinn. I promise that I'll do my best."

She blinked. "What . . . what happened to you! Your clothes are almost all gone and you're covered with blood and bruises."

"I'll tell you later," he said.

"I'd like that," she said, closing her eyes.

Longarm took her pulse and it was weak. Her wrist was so thin that he could wrap his thumb and forefinger around it and they touched. But the miracle was that Mavis Quinn had escaped the terrible Rowe family with her life, jumped in a rowboat, and landed on this same beach that he'd spotted as being his best, perhaps his only, chance of survival. And then she'd kept herself alive with this creek water, green Indian squash, and God only knew what else until now.

Longarm leaned close and whispered, "You're a real trooper, Mavis, and we're going to get through this alive . . . you and me."

"I'm sure we will," she whispered. "Now, please find me something decent to eat."

Longarm smiled and stood to his full height. He had a knife and his wits and his strength . . . or at least most of it . . . left. And now he was going to find food for them to eat and figure a way out of this deadly side canyon in the middle of Nowhere, Arizona.

Chapter 24

When the young Mormon who manned the big raft at Lees Ferry heard the distant shots, he was sitting on a rock thinking about how he might like to become a United States marshal someday and go to Denver. Oh sure, the elders of his church would discourage such a thing and even forbid it, but Jacob Young still liked to think how exciting the job would be in comparison to operating this big raft at the crossing. Heck, it would even be far more fun than becoming a farmer, for that matter.

The shots startled him. They weren't just pistol or rifle shots; a few of them were definitely from a shotgun.

And then he remembered that that awful, ugly fat woman named Gertie kept a shotgun hidden behind the plank that she called a bar top.

Jacob Young stood up and began to pace up and down the beach. He knew all about the judge and his wife going missing and about those three river guides that had gotten their throats slit. And he was pretty sure that the fat woman and her two brothers were behind the killing, which is why he had been warned to stay away from that place unless there was an emergency and he was accompanied by armed members of his church.

But something told Jacob Young that there was no time to hike up the canyon and see if he could get help. And then, when the old roan horse that the lawman had been riding came trotting down the riverside to stop beside Jacob, he was dead certain that there was a real crisis up at the saloon, store, and boat rental. And he was pretty sure that the marshal would never willingly allow his horse and saddle to run away unless he was in terrible trouble.

Jacob squared his shoulders, grabbed his hunting rifle, and swung up in the saddle.

"Giddyup!" he said, reining the big-headed roan back down the riverside.

It didn't take him more than fifteen minutes to come into sight of the saloon and store. And a moment after that he saw Wade and Orvis lying dead on the porch with the fat woman named Gertie standing howling with grief and clenching that shotgun.

Jacob tugged on his reins, and the roan went from a trot to a walk. The horse was sweating and so was Jacob as he warily eyed the scene.

When Gertie saw Jacob approaching, she cursed something, and then, by gawd, she raised her shotgun, screamed something terrible at Jacob Young, and pulled the trigger.

What happened next was almost too terrible to behold. The shotgun's barrel must have been packed with mud because it blew up in Gertie's face! Just exploded, and there was Gertie with half her face gone, falling dead as a post!

Jacob Young damned near pissed in his pants. He was shaking as he dismounted and walked over to the quivery mass that was Gertie. She moaned, jerked around for a few seconds, and then was gone.

"Oh dear God in heaven," Jacob whispered, shaking his head back and forth. "What am I goin' to do now!"

He went inside the store, and it stunk so bad he backed out. But at least the marshal's body wasn't lying in there. Had these awful people managed to kill the federal marshal then dump his body in the river?

Didn't seem too likely that Gertie alone could have dragged a man as big and heavy as the United States marshal down to the river and sunk his body with stones. And there hadn't been much time between now and the first firing of the shotgun.

Nope.

Jacob Young scratched his head and tried but failed to look at the bodies. What an ungodly mess! What had happened!

Then he started looking at tracks, and he followed a pair right on down to the river. The front of the tracks were cupped, and Jacob was pretty sure that meant that the man who'd left them had been running for his life.

"He got into the river," Jacob muttered. "He must have made it to the river!"

Jacob stood and gazed at the boiling current, and then he saw that a boat had been pulled off the beach. Its bow had left a mark anyone could see.

"He got away," Jacob reasoned aloud. "But he wasn't no river man."

Right then Jacob knew what he had to do. He unsaddled the roan and corralled it with plenty of hay before he hurried down to the river, pushed a rowboat into the current, and laid his rifle across his knees. He'd not be able to go more than a mile or two because beyond that he wouldn't be able to walk back.

But he had to go that mile or two . . . just purely had to.

A short time later, and after running a stretch of rough white water, Jacob Young rounded a bend and saw the lawman walking along the beach acting as if he'd lost something.

"Hey!" Jacob yelled, rowing powerfully toward the beach. "You all right, Marshal Long?"

Custis heard the shout over the loud water. He looked up, saw the big Mormon kid from Lees Crossing, and then laughed.

"Got any food with you!" he bellowed.

Jacob didn't answer until he'd rowed up on the beach. "Holy cow, Marshal, did you shoot those two Rowe brothers?"

"That's right, and the sister almost killed me. I swear I'm going to watch her hang."

"Ain't too much chance of that," Jacob drawled. "Danged if she didn't try to shoot me and your old horse, but her shotgun blew up in her fat face. Blew it near clean away!"

Longarm's jaw dropped. "She's dead?"

"Dead as a post, Marshal."

Custis Long grinned and clapped the Mormon kid on his broad shoulders. "Mrs. Quinn is just up the canyon a little ways, and she's almost starved to death."

"She's alive!"

"Sure is."

Jacob wiped his perspiring face. "Reckon we need to get her back upriver and feed her then."

"I reckon we do."

"River do that . . . take away most of your clothes?"

"It did for a fact."

Jacob nodded with understanding. "That big Colorado will take everything a man has or ever will have given a chance."

"I know that."

"We'd better go and help that woman." Jacob looked down at the old squash rinds. "She eat them Indian squash?"

"Tried to."

"I can't stand squash," Jacob said, turning and starting to walk up the canyon.

"Neither could she," Longarm muttered, "and she hated the pink rattlesnake meat even worse."

Jacob turned. "The woman killed a rattler down here and tried to eat it?"

"Yep. Saw its remains with my own eyes."

"Then she musta really been hungry," Jacob said. "And that's why folks need the bounty of good farmers."

"I reckon that's true," Longarm agreed as he trudged up the canyon, thinking just how fortunate he and the woman were to be alive.

Watch for

LONGARM AND THE 400 BLOWS

the 400th novel in the exciting LONGARM
series from Jove

Coming in March!

GIANT-SIZED ADVENTURE FROM AVENGING ANGEL LONGARM.

BY TABOR EVANS

M456AS0510

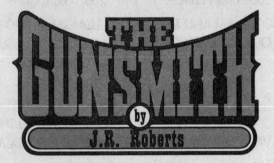

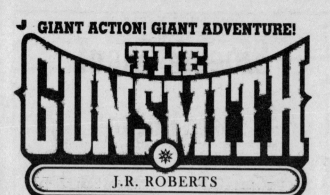

GIANT ACTION! GIANT ADVENTURE!

THE Gunsmith

J.R. ROBERTS

1825

DON'T MISS A YEAR OF

Slocum Giant
by
Jake Logan

Slocum Giant 2004:
Slocum in the Secret
Service

Slocum Giant 2005:
Slocum and the Larcenous
Lady

Slocum Giant 2006:
Slocum and the Hanging
Horse

Slocum Giant 2007:
Slocum and the Celestial
Bones

Slocum Giant 2008:
Slocum and the Town
Killers

Slocum Giant 2009:
Slocum's Great
Race

Slocum Giant 2010:
Slocum Along
Rotten Row

M457AS0510